"Award-winning Israeli novelist Sarid's latest work is a slim but powerful novel, rendered beautifully in English by translator Greenspan. . . . Propelled by the narrator's distinctive voice, the novel is an original variation on one of the most essential themes of post-Holocaust literature: While countless writers have asked the question of where, or if, humanity can be found within the profoundly inhumane, Sarid incisively shows how preoccupation and obsession with the inhumane can take a toll on one's own humanity. . . . it is, if not an indictment of Holocaust memorialization, a nuanced and trenchant consideration of its layered politics. Ultimately, Sarid both refuses to apologize for Jewish rage and condemns the nefarious forms it sometimes takes. A bold, masterful exploration of the banality of evil and the nature of revenge, controversial no matter how it is read."

KIRKUS REVIEWS, STARRED REVIEW

"Sarid's incisive critique of Holocaust memorialization, the corruption within it, and the perverse forms of nationalism it can engender is courageous. . . . anything but moralistic, it leaves the reader to draw their own conclusions about the complex politics of Holocaust memorialization and its many layers of irony. . . . Ultimately, he presents Jewish rage unapologetically, and that, too, is radical. *The Memory Monster* presents challenges to all sorts of unspoken norms about Jewish culture's treatment of the Holocaust; it will likely unsettle if not anger people across the political spectrum, and therein lies its value."

MIRANDA COOPER, *LA REVIEW OF BOOKS*

"The short, but powerful novel raises the question of how far we let the horrors of the past infiltrate our present day lives. . . . *The*

Memory Monster is not an easy book to read but its message is important to hear."

ELLIS SHUMAN, *THE TIMES OF ISRAEL*

"The most brilliant and chilling novel I have read in a very long time."

JILL PELÁEZ BAUMGAERTNER, *THE CHRISTIAN CENTURY*

"*The Memory Monster* is one of the great Israeli novels to have been published in translation in recent years. Sarid's book is wonderfully subversive, darkly humorous; riveting, challenging, and thought-provoking. The voice—captured well in English by Yardenne Greenspan—is finely balanced, teetering on the edge as the memory monster sinks its teeth deeper and deeper into Sarid's protagonist. *The Memory Monster* is a novel that demands to be read and deserves our attention."

LIAM HOARE, FATHOM

"Reading *The Memory Monster*, which is written as a report to the director of Yad Vashem, felt like both an extremely intimate experience and an eerily clinical Holocaust history lesson. Perfectly treading the fine line between these two approaches, Sarid creates a haunting exploration of collective memory and an important commentary on humanity. How do we remember the Holocaust? What tolls do we pay to carry on memory? This book hit me viscerally, emotionally, and personally. *The Memory Monster* is brief, but in its short account Sarid manages to lay bare the tensions between memory and morals, history and nationalism, humanity and victimhood. An absolute must-read."

JULIA DEVARTI, LITERATI BOOKSTORE (ANN ARBOR, MI)

"The first English translation of a book by Israeli novelist Yishai Sarid appears at an opportune time. Restless Books is publishing Yardenne Greenspan's able translation of *The Memory Monster* amid a fresh rise of fascism in the West. . . . Numerous powerful passages evoke [the narrator's] increasingly vivid interior experiences of what happened at the camps. . . . The book feels like real life in its humble details, but even more so in its implied conclusion that no ultimate actions, no final solutions, are ever truly available to us. . . . It makes a valuable contribution to the present generation of Holocaust literature. It adds to the hope that the memory of the monster may linger unto the nth generation."

JON SOBEL, BLOGCRITICS

"*The Memory Monster* is shattering, brilliant, disturbing, and very important. Sarid's background as a lawyer makes the narrator's arguments—and his falling apart—all the more disturbing when his logic fails. How can the horrors of the Holocaust be taught, remembered? A powerful novel."

LYNNE TILLMAN, AUTHOR OF MEN AND APPARITIONS

"This is a moving and important addition to the literature of the period, alongside writers like Primo Levi, confirming that the horrors of war extend to the next generation who are so deeply and ineluctably affected by the events of the past."

MELANIE FLEISHMAN,
CENTER FOR FICTION (BROOKLYN, NY)

"Sarid depicts how these issues surface not only at the individual level, but at the national one. Recollection of the Holocaust is a core value of the State of Israel, and many moments in the book point to a problematic relationship to that memory. . . . The implication is that for a people who experienced utter powerlessness during the Nazi era, the enduring lessons about power and the use of force can remain complicated and unsettling."

"[A] record of a breakdown, an impassioned consideration of memory and its risks, and a critique of Israel's use of the Holocaust to shape national identity. . . . Sarid's unrelenting examination of how narratives of the Holocaust are shaped makes for much more than the average confessional tale."

"In Yishai Sarid's dark, thoughtful novel *The Memory Monster*, a Holocaust historian struggles with the weight of his profession. . . . *The Memory Monster* is a novel that pulls no punches in its exploration of the responsibility—and the cost—of holding vigil over the past."

"[I]t is perhaps the most important novel about the Holocaust and Holocaust memory to have been written in the last ten years."

The Investigation of Captain Erez

Limassol

Naomi's Kindergarten

The Third

Victorious

YISHAI SARID

THE MEMORY
MONSTER

A NOVEL

Translated from the Hebrew by
Yardenne Greenspan

RESTLESS BOOKS
BROOKLYN, NEW YORK

Originally published in hardcover and ebook by Restless Books in 2020.
First trade paperback edition: September 2021

Paperback ISBN: 9781632060600
Library of Congress Control Number: 2021937599

Cover design by Na Kim
Set in Garibaldi by Tetragon, London

Printed in the United States of America
1 3 5 7 9 10 8 6 4 2

Restless Books, Inc.
232 3rd Street, Suite A101
Brooklyn, NY 11215

www.restlessbooks.org
publisher@restlessbooks.org

THE MEMORY
MONSTER

DEAR CHAIRMAN of the Board of Yad Vashem,

The following is a report of what happened there.

I've been informed that you have been expecting this report, and I too am eager to provide it. I appreciate the opportunity to earn your trust.

At first, I tried to separate myself from the report and convey it in a clean, academic fashion, without bringing in my own personality or my private life, which, in and of themselves, are nothing worthy of discussion. But after writing only a few lines, I realized that was impossible. I was the vessel inside which the story lived. If I widened the cracks until I broke, the story would be lost, too.

Please know that I have always looked up to you. I have participated in your discussions and consultations, and I've been tasked by you with several important assignments, including this final project. I will never forget your moving words at my book launch. I have helped you in

3

every way I could, and I do not remember ever exchanging a mundane word with you. For this I have no grievance. The burden you carry is great. I recall the beautiful view of the Jerusalem Forest from your office window, the smell of the stone walls, and the fine fabric of your clothing. I've always seen myself as your loyal emissary. I see before me your wise face and I address you now as the official representative of memory.

I found myself specializing in Holocaust research out of practical considerations. After being honorably discharged from military service and after the end of the customary traveling and indecision period, I enrolled in a history and international relations program. I yearned to find work as a diplomat. I thought I'd be happier living abroad. I knew international service had lost some of its cachet and was no longer essential in this digital age, but I saw this as an advantage. I envisioned myself sitting at a café in some tropical city in a light-colored suit, spending my days in elegant languidness, living on a modest yet respectable salary paid by the state. I had no aspirations to be a lead player, someone who has streets and squares named after them. I loved reading books about historical figures and events; they soothed me because everything in them was final and complete. Nothing could change.

Fictional stories were in the control of a single person's whims, and made me restless.

In my second year at university I took the Ministry of Foreign Affairs tests. I was twenty-four years old and passed the first round—the written exam—with ease. In the second round, which I was summoned to attend a few weeks later, the testers had us perform group assignments, all sorts of clever games, and finally one-on-one interviews. As the day wore on, I could feel myself running aground. I didn't need to wait for the letter to know I had failed.

For a while, I considered leaving it all and going east, to Thailand. My future was closing in on me. But financial and familial considerations (my father had fallen ill around that time) stopped me from pursuing that notion. Once my dream of diplomatic service died, I quit the international relations program, which I had no real interest in, and majored in history alone.

I loved studying history: writing papers, doing research, spending hours in the library with old texts, taking a break at the cafeteria, coming back. I moved around calmly and adopted the pretense of gravity. Naturally, I continued on to a master's degree and lost my anonymity after receiving accolades for a senior thesis I wrote for a class taught by the dean of the university himself. He took me under his wing and offered me a job as one of his teaching assistants. I became a history apprentice and was proud of my new status. The dean discussed future opportunities, studying abroad. I could see myself sitting in front of a fireplace in Oxford or Boston, aging with honor, and was no longer so upset about being rejected by the Ministry of Foreign Affairs.

I was fearful of modern history, which reminded me of a terrifying waterfall rumbling with awful ferocity. I was looking for a peaceful life, one that revolved around ancient times whose history was open and shut, which did not awaken any intense emotions in anyone. I considered specializing in the history of the Far East, but for that I had to study Chinese or Japanese, and I didn't have much of a knack for languages. I wanted to stay far away from the disasters and calamities of our own people, guessing from the start the danger that lay in wait for me there. But when I met Ruth, and knew we were headed toward marriage, I had to start thinking in practical terms. When I thought more about it I realized that, seemingly, I had all of human history laid out before me, but that in fact there were only few open veins available to me. Job openings at universities were rare and quickly occupied by senior professors, and new jobs were given to outside hires— basically subcontractors—at hunger salaries.

One day, the dean told me that the Intelligence Corps was on the lookout for Iran experts and willing to fund doctoral studies in Persian history for a suitable candidate. The condition, the dean emphasized, was to commit to seven years of standing army service. I knew this kind of service meant sitting in an office at the central military base in Tel Aviv, not in the tanks I manned during mandatory duty, but the thought of being drafted again caused me to lose a few nights of sleep, after which I informed the dean I wasn't interested. What's more, this specialization required, once again, learning a difficult foreign language. The dean understood, and said that meant I had one last realistic option for continuing my life as a historian in Israel— getting a PhD in Holocaust Studies.

I was afraid. I wanted to continue to cruise through life as on a calm lake, clear of worry and turmoil. I made a few barren attempts to evade this burden, and almost succeeded: a fine university in Perth, Australia accepted me to a doctoral program in Medieval European History, offering housing and a teaching position. But Ruth wasn't thrilled about the idea of moving to Australia, and we already had a wedding date set. Had we gone to those sunny beaches, with pints of beer served from four in the afternoon, our shared fate might have been different.

I gave in.

I came to the dean's office and announced I was prepared to harness myself to the memory chariot. From
the moment I did so, almost everything changed for the
better. I received a small fellowship, a donation from an
American Jewish family, which was sufficient to cover our
modest lifestyle. I began to study German, and within a
few months was able to read official SS letters. My profi-
ciency remained fairly basic. I never tried to read Heine or
Goethe. I gobbled up as many books and studies as I could
find. That was my strength—the ability to digest large
quantities of written material in a short amount of time.
I was drawn to the technical details of annihilation: the
mechanism, the manpower, the method. I delved deeper
and deeper, until my dissertation topic had formulated
and received approval from my advisor. I was on track.

*Unity and Distinction in German Death Camps' Methods
of Actions During World War II.* That was the topic of my
dissertation. I compared extermination processes in each
camp— Chelmno, Belzec, Treblinka, Sobibor, Majdanek,
and Auschwitz (of course the latter two were different,
being labor camps as well as death camps)—and parsed
them out. I took a close-up look at the stages performed at
each camp, from the moment prisoners descended from
the trains, through undressing, the collection of clothes
and luggage, the false presentations given by Germans to

keep their victims at ease, the hair shaving, the march to the gas chambers, the structures of gas chambers and the type of gas used, the manner of assembling people inside them, the process of extermination, the pulling of gold teeth and the cavity search, the disposal of bodies, the division of labor between different stations, and so on and so forth. I searched these for similarities and dissimilarities. Of course, each step was made up of countless small details that also entailed variations of their own. I read hundreds of books and testimonies about life and death in the camps, possibly thousands, and delved as deeply as I could into raw documents in an attempt to clarify equivocal details. There was a plethora of information, and I navigated my way through it with a steady hand. My flow charts branched out, but I never lost control of them. I first organized my facts carefully—Ruth assisted me in creating specialized comparison files—and then investigated the academic question of the variety that existed in methods of action; a surprising deviation from absolute unity, as one might have expected from an organization and a task of this nature

At the same time, to make a living, I began working as a tour guide at Yad Vashem. You yourself were the head of the committee that gave me the position. I recall your demeanor and the awe you inspired in me. You asked me why I wanted to be a guide, and if I was aware of the extreme mental burden the work entailed. I answered with a half-truth, explaining that this was an extraordinary opportunity for a historian to make real-life use of his profession, disseminating his knowledge publicly. I didn't say my wife was pregnant and I had to provide for my growing family. I told you I was in the midst of working on my dissertation, and that I had plenty of detailed information on the techniques of extermination. In my CV, I included my experience teaching a gunnery course at the Armored Corps School, and mentioned that later, at university, I served as a teaching assistant to the dean of the history faculty. You asked me to present you with a truncated version of the story of the Warsaw Ghetto Uprising, the way I would tell it if you were a school student. I must have made a good impression, because the very next day I got a call informing me the job was mine. I didn't take your warnings about the emotional strain too seriously because I had never suffered true emotional turmoil in my life, and thought I was immune. I burst into the field like a young bull and began working right away as a guide at the museum, the Garden of the Righteous Among the Nations, and in classrooms. I showered the children with my knowledge. I had a knack for it. I aspired to give them a clear-cut summary of the big picture rather than bombard them with endless details, to take hold of several plotlines. I couldn't convey every subplot—the kids would get totally lost. Some children from one of the first classes I guided told me that thanks to me they could truly understand, for the very first time, this whole enormous story of the Holocaust.

I was hardworking and always well-prepared for lectures. I never showed up unprepared. I worked from the assumption that they knew nothing and that I bore the entire responsibility of teaching this memory to them. I explained the roots of anti-Semitism, both traditional and modern, the rise of the Nazis, a bit of Hitler's biography and the biographies of his first emissaries, the start of the war, the negation of rights, imprisonment in ghettos, banishments, extermination.

Sometimes I was enchanted by the interesting face of a girl or boy or an intelligent question asked, but mostly classes came and went without leaving any special impression. I remember that once, you dropped in unexpectedly to listen to me give a lecture to high school students from Rehovot or Gedera. You sat in the back and signaled for me to carry on, and I wanted to impress you. There was a blueprint of Treblinka on the screen, and I flowed between stations with ease until I reached the burning of bodies in large decay pits. A few minutes later you nodded and walked out. Then the wing manager came to see me. She said you were impressed by my knowledge, but thought I lacked some emotion and personal attention to victims. *I'm a historian*, I thought, *not a social worker*, but I promised I would take that into consideration and try to correct my ways.

I went to Poland for the first time to write my doctoral dissertation and see the places about which I'd read tens of thousands of pages. My advisor, the Chair of Holocaust Studies at the university, was supposed to go with me. He had some complicated connections there. But he pulled a muscle in his back the night before the flight; might have even slipped a disc. So I went alone. I rented a car at the airport and spent two weeks driving between camps, pouncing at them hungrily, and returning with hundreds of photographs and notebooks filled with sketches.

Everything fell into place during this visit. I understood exactly what I was seeing, and this understanding brought on a kind of intellectual elation. My dissertation was infinitely improved.

A few months later I returned to Poland for a delegation guide course. The sites were already familiar to me, and I almost felt at home. After I'd been formally authorized as a tour guide, I started making bookings and traveled to Poland more and more frequently. I made a few thousand shekels for each trip, finally earning a decent living for my little family: Ruth and our child, Ido.

Before too long, during high school heritage trip season, I would be away from home for a month at a time, sometimes longer, because there wasn't enough time to come home between trips. Ruth and the baby got used to it. We had no other choice. I don't know if you've ever been on one of those high school delegations: flying with them in the middle of the night, spending seven or eight days with them on the road, standing before them and explaining over and over again what happened in those forests, those ghettos, those camps, trying to carve a path into their expressionless faces, their minds filled with iPhone flickers. I don't know if you've ever tried to illustrate death to them, providing them with data and facts, numbers and names, or had them follow you around, wrapped in flags, singing the national anthem near the gas chambers, saying the Kaddish prayer by the piles of ashes, lighting candles in memory of the children in the pits, performing all sorts of made-up rituals, working so hard to squeeze out a tear. I've asked myself so many times whether you've ever experienced this first-hand.

The tour always began at the Warsaw Cemetery. Mr. Chairman, I tell you, it would be best to leave that part out. None of them knows who I. L. Peretz is and why he received such an impressive monument. I suppose he used to be an important author, but I don't know anyone who's ever read any of his books. They have no idea what Esperanto is, either, or that a man named Zamenhof was its creator. And they're right, the whole Esperanto ordeal was a bust. We try to present them with a magnificent culture, but the truth is the Jews who lived in Poland didn't build cathedrals or write symphonies. Most of them were petty merchants, simple people who ate herring and listened to klezmer music and lived in cabins. Toward the end, some of them were doctors or lawyers—they were among the darker-skinned people who lived in the east, the ones who murdered Jesus. The kids wander among the tombstones, tired after their red-eye flight, unsure whether it's too early to wrap themselves with an Israeli flag, answering an automatic "Amen" when the teacher says the Kaddish prayer over every important grave. They're cold, and all they want is to go to the hotel and enjoy a little bit of that "abroad" feeling.

After the cemetery we take them to the old Jewish quarter, to the dispatch quad at Umschlagplatz, and to the rebels' bunker on Mila 18. "They were hardly older than you are now," I tell them, "with almost no weapons at all; only a few Molotov cocktails, some hand grenades, and some guns. And with those measly resources, they were able to block a German military brigade for nearly a month."

I stood before them, trying to convey to them the suffering and the heroism, holding strong to all of your messages, never deviating right or left. I was a good boy, doing my best to invade past those jeans and leggings and curls and ponytails and heavy coats, that flat, fast talking, the indifferent eyes, and the phones. To invade their hearts and their minds. I never felt like I truly succeeded, because I didn't love them enough. I know that now.

Nights at hotels are a teacher's worst nightmare. The last thing they want is to see a headline in tomorrow's newspaper describing Israeli students acting out in Poland, trashing rooms, getting drunk, calling prostitutes. To prevent this kind of behavior, the teachers patrol the halls, pressing their ears against doors, threatening the children with terrible punishments, forbidding them from leaving the hotel. When morning comes, their eyes are red with lack of sleep. But usually nothing happens. The kids roam the lobby, at worst ordering a Coke, then shower in their rooms using the hotel shampoo and soap and play sad songs on their guitars, going to sleep like good little children at lights out. True, on occasion we get some disruptive kids—not really kids at all, but rather young pimps with their girls, small loudspeakers blaring

Mediterranean music all night long as a revenge against gentiles and Ashkenazi Jews, ordering room service without paying, leaving their rooms filthy. And then, what a commotion ensues! Their teachers summon me to save the day and I come to offer help, though it isn't part of my job description. I talk to the wild animals, I know how to do that, reach an agreement with the receptionist regarding reasonable compensation, and calm the agitated parents. A weak flicker in my mind tells me that these wild types are capable of murder, but they have a hard time with commands. They know to reject them, evade them, manipulating their way out of them, smuggling little bottles of vodka into their rooms, making noise in the middle of the night, but perhaps on the deciding day they wouldn't turn in their neighbor, refusing orders, unlike the good kids, who would obey immediately, because for them a law is a law.

Usually we went to Majdanek on the second day—a long drive east on a road where Krupp tanks used to pass on their way to occupy additional living territory for the German people. Fields sprawled from one horizon to the next, planted with cabbage and turnip. I know what a tank is and am familiar with the magnificent feeling of driving without resistance, without stopping, without hitting the brakes, in the belly of a racing metal beast, living as one of its organs. Twice on the way we stopped at gas stations for food and drink or else the kids got antsy. As we know, the Germans didn't get a chance to destroy the camp before the Russian invasion, and to this day it remains untouched on the outskirts of Lublin, exposed for all to see from the highway. Majdanek hits you with everything all at once. Two small gas chambers are located just by the gate, on the right. One of them was filled with carbon monoxide through a pipe that emerged from a tank's motor, while the other was filled with Zyklon B from cans. Between a hundred thousand and two hundred thousand people died there; no one knows the exact number. Compared to other camps, that isn't much, but everything is still there, the entire operation. Even the crematorium remains whole on a hill, inside a house with a chimney, German ovens in mint condition. Beside the house were the killing pits into which 20,000 Jews were shot on one day during the harvest festivities, when the Germans wanted a good time. For some reason, in Majdanek, of all places, on the few hundred meters' walk from the gas chambers to the dirt monument and the crematoriums, I heard them talking about Arabs, wrapped in their flags and whispering, *The Arabs, that's what we should do to the Arabs*. Not always, not in all groups, but often enough for me to remember it. I pretended I didn't hear them; it was none of my business, let the teachers handle it. But I heard it, Mr. Chairman, I can't lie. When they see this simple killing mechanism, which can be easily recreated in any place and at any time, it inspires practical thinking. And they're still children, it's natural, they find it hard to stop. Adults think the same things, but they keep it to themselves. Toward the end, on my last few trips, I gave my little speech outside the crematorium rather than join them inside. I didn't want to hear what they were saying in there.

In Lublin we also visited the Chachmei Lublin Yeshiva, which now operates an odd hotel, decorated with Jewish symbols. The synagogue can be entered through a side gate, where one pays the Polish guard a few zloty. Religious kids with knitted yarmulkes like to pray there. I stand on the side, listening. Sometimes I like the tune, or I relate to one line or another. Later, at the old city, at the foot of the fort, I read to them from *The Magician of Lublin*. It's rare to find one among them who has read Bashevis Singer—there I go again, bad-mouthing the youth, but I promised to tell the truth.

Other than Jewish history, not much is left of this eastern city, what a bore. Tourists rarely go there, aside from war buffs. This building used to house Gestapo headquarters; this villa used to be the home of Odilo Globocnik, the SS officer responsible for Operation Reinhard; this backyard is where Jews were forced to perform hard labor. Those are the kinds of attractions Lublin has to offer. The population is pale and forlorn. Black people and Arabs are not allowed to enter Poland. Borders are closed to them, and the State of Israel helps them achieve their goals with all sorts of electronic equipment we provide them. And it's working. All you see on the streets are white faces, all alike, unnerving.

At night, I sat at the hotel bar and drank. Otherwise I wouldn't be able to sleep. Often, my nerves were so shot that it was as if the operation was happening right then and I was taking part in the planning, the handling, the maintaining of schedules. Sometimes I had chest pain, eyelid twitching. I wasn't calm. I looked forward to my moments of drinking at the bar at the end of the day, hidden from view, sitting in a remote corner so as not to be seen. Sometimes some rebellious teacher who also felt the need for some distance joined me. You always had to keep an eye on the kids, worrying about what they might do, to make sure they didn't try to flee the hotel. It was a week-long anxiety attack.

Whenever a female teacher sat down beside me at the bar, I felt like a hairy carnivorous plant. I wanted to swallow them whole. They wanted me to comfort them after the difficult sights of the day, to explain to them how it was possible. Later, after we'd had a few drinks, they asked about my life, about my wife. It happened on occasion that we took it even further. A spark lit up in our eyes, and we had all the necessary emotional excuses, a need for warmth and love.

The first time it happened, the teacher had a long face and sad Jewish eyes. She wanted me to explain to her personally why they did it. She just couldn't wrap her mind around it. She had too much to drink. I gently told her she was overreacting. I don't care, she said with the light-headedness of a drunk. She couldn't have the children see her like that, and the only solution was to take her to my room, which was on another floor, and let her rest there until her intoxication wore out. She asked to take a shower and then came out of the bathroom half naked. I truly tried to avoid it, but she fell asleep in my bed and only woke up in the morning. I'd hoped she'd come back over the next few days, but she'd sobered up. I don't want to share the other incidents; it happened one or two more times, it doesn't matter right now. That really wasn't the kind of guy I was. Usually, three shots of vodka were enough for me to fall asleep in the old Gestapo hotel in Lublin.

On the first trips, I was always teamed up with the same survivor, an old man named Eliezer. A short, energetic, friendly guy. He liked talking to the kids, answering their questions, pulling them in. He was eleven years old when he fled his hometown the night before the Germans sent the Jews to die in Belzec. His parents told him to run away by himself. His siblings were too young. He lived in the forest until the Partisans found him. His father was a tailor, so he was able to mend their clothing. He also cooked for them, and on occasion even joined them in sabotaging train tracks. The students ate up his words with bated breath. Though I recognized all sorts of holes in his narrative, it was mostly reliable, so I didn't interrogate or make comments. I've never heard a survivor's story that was completely whole.

Eliezer's main shortcoming was that he'd never spent any time at a camp, having lived out most of the war in the forest. Still, he liked to talk about the camps, the youth, and the State of Israel, speaking proudly and hopefully about topics that had nothing to do with his personal experience. But the students and the teachers loved him, and I didn't intervene. The survivors from the camps were few and infirm, and Eliezer was just fine. I sat next to him during long bus rides. He told me about his children and grandchildren, about the fine workshop he'd started when he came to Israel, and about other matters related to commerce and family. His clothes smelled pleasantly of old age. We made a good team. He made up for my lack of emotion. We had a regular lineup: I delivered the facts, and he added the personal touch. It worked perfectly until one day Eliezer fell at home and broke his hip. He couldn't join the trips while he recovered, and never came back after that.

I went to visit him. He was lying in bed, pumped up with painkillers. All at once, he'd become an invalid, his wife spoon-feeding him oatmeal. I stayed briefly, and never saw him again. He was very hard to replace. I made use of your information resources in order to set up meetings with some survivors, traveling quite a bit over Israel to see them. I interviewed them, tried to figure them out, and to convince the suitable candidates to join me. I explained the importance of giving testament to our youth, to transfer memory to them directly, but success was limited. Most of them were not healthy enough to withstand the trip. Some had lost their lucidity of thought and recollection, suffering from some level of senility. Others were afraid of the trauma, refusing to return, which was understandable. I suspected that a few used to be kapos or collaborators and hid the truth their entire lives. Why would they open this can of worms now, so close to their own graves?

I worked for months, trying to convince a survivor named Yohanan to join me. He lived up north and was a retired construction engineer. His entire life he vehemently refused to go back, but after his wife died, he was plagued with yearning for his parents and sister, who had been murdered, and for their old home. I convinced him to join and promised we would visit his hometown. He told me briefly about how he was fifteen when he was taken away. His sister was seventeen at the time, and both of them passed selection. Their mother did not pass due to her skin disease, and their father had been taken to a labor camp and disappeared months earlier. "I'd forgotten their faces years ago," he told me, "and now they are back. I can see them so clearly."

I kept my promise. On the way to Krakow, we got off the highway and drove to his town, which was identical to thousands of others in Poland and tens of thousands of others all over Europe. The bus stopped at the town square, across from the church, the butcher shop, and the bakery. I told them—based on my research—that the church was built by the landowning noble during a period of healthy crops. This noble had also accused five Jewish men of mixing the blood of Christian babies into matzah meal. Their sentence was carried out by two horses that pulled each man in opposite directions. Nevertheless, Jews continued to live there. They were loathed and harassed, but they were part of the landscape.

Yohanan pointed to a remote corner of the square, where the synagogue used to be. We discovered it was now a small bank. We went inside and I pointed out the spot where the Holy Ark would have been. The bank teller got nervous, speaking in agitated Polish. One of the hotheaded boys answered her, and a brawl almost ensued. The branch manager came out of his office, gesturing for everyone to settle down. I explained in English that Yohanan used to live in this town and that this place used to be the synagogue. The bank manager hummed and said, "Welcome, welcome," but his body language told me he wanted us out.

From there, Yohanan led us toward his old house. I could see him searching for clues in the old trees, the yards. He stumbled over the broken sidewalk, turned onto a neglected street, paused in front of a small house, and said: "It was here. This is where we used to live."

We glanced inside through the window. Darkness and abandon. Nobody answered the door. One of the teachers cried. The kids surrounded Yohanan as he told them about his family, choking on his tears. He was beside himself. The children comforted him, the teachers hugged him, they were all so wonderful.

When we returned to the church square a few Polish people stared at us. The bank manager stepped outside as well. Tourists never came to this town, and it had certainly

not seen Jews since the war. One of the passersby, reek-
ing of booze, came over to talk to us. Go argue about a
thousand years of history with a drunk. I gave him some
money, so he didn't think Jews were cheap, and he waved
the money in front of the others. We left.

The next day, having paid my debt to Yohanan, we
went to Auschwitz. Even the worst-behaved kids can't
help but be awed at Auschwitz. The branding does the
job. Yohanan was feeling weak, and I could see he had
trouble walking, his face expressionless. His personal
story was meant to imbue all the abandoned structures
and objects we would see throughout the day with meaning, and I hoped he would do his job. At first, as usual,
we toured the first camp—Auschwitz I. The students
had trouble figuring the place out. It didn't contain the
wooden sheds they'd seen in pictures, but better-looking
stone structures that used to serve as Polish military barracks. Only inside can one see the torture rooms, the piles
of hair and prosthetics, the original gas chamber, and
the crematorium. Yohanan told me awkwardly that he'd
never been there; it didn't resemble anything he could
remember. I assured him that he hadn't been here, but
in Auschwitz II, better known as Birkenau. Two students
supported him, but he insisted on walking on his own,
using a cane.

From there, we rode for two or three minutes to Birkenau. There's that moment when the camp suddenly sprawls before you—electric fences, sheds, train tracks, gate. It's real, it's the place. You can actually touch the place where humanity was murdered. I saw Yohanan's hands shaking, his mouth moving inaudibly, and I realized I'd made a mistake. I shouldn't have talked him into it; the memories were too strong. The children wrapped themselves with their flags and took pictures of the gate and the tracks running through it. I led them to the ramp, right near the model train car, where I always start my lecture. That was where the selection process took place: To the right, those sent to immediate death, an average seventy-five percent of each transport; to the left, those found suitable for death by hard labor. They went to the sheds, the undressing, the shaving, the tattooing of numbers.

"I can see the fire," Yohanan said, staring into the distance, toward the end of the road. "Tell them," I implored. They were all standing around him, waiting for him to speak.

"Mother was taken there right away," he said, trembling. "She had a red rash because we didn't have water for bathing. When we saw the smoke coming out of the chimney, we knew it was Mother. There was no need for explanations. We were taken that way." He pointed toward the sheds beyond the tracks. "First my sister, then me. I saw her in the distance. She was taller than me. That was it. What did I do there, in the sheds, the shitters, the quarries, you ask? Who cares? What difference does it make? I knew why I didn't want to come here. I knew they would start the fire and have me jump into it. I didn't do anything to deserve to live, kids, don't let anyone tell you that kind of nonsense. It hurts, oh, it hurts too much," he said. There was no point in trying to get him to say more. He had made his sacrifice to the Memory Monster.

I ended the tour there. We didn't go to the sheds or the ruins of the gas chambers. It was as if his mother and sister were suffocating in there right at that very moment, writhing, turning blue, pissing and shitting themselves. Maybe they were having their periods. Maybe the Sonderkommando pulled them outside and checked for diamonds in their mouths and between their legs. It was happening as we spoke, and we couldn't stay there.

The group rebelled. The school principal tried to persuade me, offering to have someone walk Yohanan outside and sit with him on the bus while we continued the tour. There was a rustle, disappointed stomping. The girls were wearing booties, and the boys clumsy sneakers. But my mind was made up. I brought him here, and I would get him out. He would not be staying in Auschwitz a moment longer.

We returned to Krakow. When we arrived at the hotel our delegation doctor examined Yohanan and gave him a tranquilizer because he was still very upset. I arranged with the travel agency to have him on the first flight to Warsaw the next morning, from which he would continue to Israel. Please don't worry, the children didn't miss a thing—the next morning we returned to Birkenau without him to complete our tour.

"Hate," I tried to explain to them inside the model shed, among the bunks, "and evil, and economy. Economy, hate, and evil—that's what happened here." For the first time, I dared to veer from your regular script, the one all guides use, and my voice was shaking. "This is where the illusion we call humankind was erased. Look at yourselves, look at your friends. What are you? Hunks of flesh. Have you ever cooked a cow? If you have, you've seen the tendons, the blood vessels, the tissue. Have you ever fried a fish? Have you removed the intestines, seen the dead eyes? That's what you are. If there's anything inside of you, other than guts, it's lusts and ugly urges, worms with aspirations. But for the sake of economy, let us utilize the animal energy that remains inside of you. You aren't strong African men, accustomed to hard work, and so your demise will be quick, pathetic, ridiculous. Your existence wounds the earth. Your appearance, the cunning way you talk, are an insult to humanity."

They looked at me, scared. What side was I on? Why was I saying those hideous things? I had to shock them. I couldn't carry on with those serene, forlorn explanations, without real protest. Later on, we paused at the ruins of extermination buildings 1 and 2, about a kilometer away from the ramp. "They arrived by foot, leaving heavy loads by the train cars. Seventy-five to eighty percent of the people on each transport were murdered on the spot." I had to make them understand this: the story of those who survived is a footnote. The real story is that of the immediate deaths that were never marked, never registered, never tattooed. Straight into the gas chambers.

I stood before them over the underground undressing hall with the shaved roof, like a picked-over scab, underneath all rot. Perpendicular to that is the gas chamber, an enormous rectangle. Everything is still screaming there, those rectangles crying at us. *How can you not see?* There's a mother, a grandfather, a child, from here they take the steps down, this is where the hangers used to be, and the benches, and the signs pointing the way to the showers. The Sonderkommandos walked among them, promising cake and hot beverages after the shower. Here and there the Germans administered some clubbing, as little as possible so that a riot didn't ensue, complicating the operation, requiring more manpower. It would make things messy, bloody. I couldn't scream it, I could only give them the facts, calmly, with restrained grief.

Sometimes, if weather permitted, we went as far as the new extermination buildings that had been built in 1944 to handle the unusually high number of transports from Hungary. It was like touring a nature reserve: waterbirds floated in small ponds, large trees swayed gracefully in the wind, small wildflowers dotted the spring grass. Nature sounds. The Germans and the Sonderkommando Jews, the extermination team, were disconnected from the rest of the world. Transports arrived two or three times a day, were taken to undress, shoved into gas chambers, two thousand people at once. A Red Cross car arrived, a German man stepped out of it and tossed in a single can of Zyklon B. The killing process lasted twenty-five minutes. When the steel door was opened they were all twisted around each other, deformed, filthy, the floor covered with their excrement.

The Jewish slaves quickly cleaned the interior, evacuated the dead transport, checked their mouths, cut the women's hair (this was in stark contrast to other camps, where the shearing took place before the murder), placed them inside the ovens, fat woman beside a skinny man, or woman–child–man, making sure there was enough fat to make the entire bundle burn. There were a few such fatty bursts of work every day, but for the most part, after they and their remnants were consumed and while the camp waited for the next transport to arrive, there was European peace and quiet and time to eat and rest.

Wherever we went, they sang the anthem. In Treblinka in front of the monument. In Auschwitz on the platform, in the forest death sites, at the Anielewicz bunker at Ulica Miła 18. They spent most of their time in Poland cloaked in flags, singing.

I talked to a teacher who had organized one of the delegations and asked her gently if we could cut down a bit. It sort of cheapens the anthem when you sing it two, three times a day, dozens of times a week.

She looked at me, puzzled. "That's what comforts them," she said. "It's our victory song. Without it, what do we have left? Despair. We don't want them coming home in despair. We want to fill them with hope."

I didn't want to argue with that. I could have, but there was no point. She was right.

They didn't hate the Germans, the kids in my groups; not at all, not even close. The murderers barely registered in the narrative they created for themselves. They sang sad songs, wrapped themselves in flags, and said prayers for the ascent of the souls of the victims, as if their death had been a divine decree, but never pointed an accusing finger at the perpetrators. They hated the Polish much more. When we walked around the streets in cities and villages, whenever we met the local population, they would mutter words of hatred at them, about the pogroms they had committed, their collaboration, their anti-Semitism. But it's hard for us to hate people like the Germans. Look at photos from the war. Let's call a spade a spade: they looked totally cool in those uniforms, on their bikes, at ease, like male models on billboards. We'll never forgive the Arabs for the way they look, with their stubble and their brown pants that go wide at the bottom, their houses without whitewash and the open sewers on the streets, the kids with pink-eye. But that fair, clean, European look makes you want to emulate them. That's one part of it.

The other part, intentionally and successfully planned by the Germans, was the fact that they committed their murder spree on Polish soil so they could keep Germany beautiful, clean, and well-organized. They kicked all the trash over to the east, to remote organic waste sites, where the stink wouldn't disrupt culture and progress.

Sophisticated tourists can visit Dachau or the formation grounds in Nuremberg or even the Olympic stadium in Berlin, but the real, appealing, sadistic stuff is in the east, where a tourist with an eye for detail can still recognize a bone peeking from the dirt when it rains. In the Black Forest, where Israelis go for some R & R on family vacations, the soil is pure. That's how the Germans planned it. And what can I say? It worked.

The third element is of course the big money they paid the State of Israel and the other perks that help us forget.

And one last thing, which has slowly permeated me over the years, is the invisible admiration of the murder; the decisiveness and ruthlessness, the audacity, the final, focused, and cruel act, after which there is nothing but silence.

Please, don't take this to mean I hated these kids. In them, I saw my exposed reflection. I attributed to them everything that had gone through my head, tormenting me. I tried to make up for this with my knowledge. Each group had a few members with wise, sensitive eyes, whom I tried to enrich. I told them over the microphone about the German yearning for the green landscape seen through the windows of the bus, about their longing for the glory days of Teutonic knights in Eastern Europe, and their desire to return to the cities those knights had founded, to regain their status as a nation of peasants and warriors, a nation of strong, maternal, fertile women.

Most of them were too loud to hear me. Their faces were glued to their phones, busy texting and playing flashing games. Only a few listened.

"Have a seat, relax," a school principal once told me, seeing how hard I was working and taking pity on me. "That's more than they need to know."

According to procedure, I was supposed to have heart-to-hearts with them at the hotel every evening, processing the difficult experiences of the day together. They were exhausted and craved some free time, and the only thing keeping them from skipping these sit-downs was their fear of the teachers and the gravity of the topic at hand. It was usually the girls who spoke during those talks, about their feelings, the sadness they'd felt during the day, while the boys said nothing, fixing their eyes on the floor, waiting for it to be over. I have to admit, I wasn't up for the task. I pretended to contain their emotions, nodded gravely, but in truth I was yearning to be at that dark corner of the bar, wrapping up my day.

I didn't believe what the children said in these public emotional inquiries. My ears were pricked to their secret conversations, in the backstage of ceremonies, between the seats of the bus, on footpaths, around the table during meals. That's where different thoughts, a different agenda, just grazing the surface, flowed from the back of the mind to the front of the mouth, between the teeth that sprayed out syllables. *Ashkenazis*, I heard them saying on more than one occasion, *are the forefathers of left-wingers*. They weren't able to protect their wives and children, collaborated with the murderers, they weren't real men, didn't know how to hit back, cowards, softies, letting the Arabs have their way. I could hear their gloating, and I could hear them telling each other in private that the Ashkenazis were not innocent victims. There was a reason they were killed, just look at what they did to the Mizrahi Jews, nobody likes a snake. Yes, I heard that kind of talk too, Mr. Chairman, I cannot lie. Someone needs to investigate this phenomenon. I let myself off the hook with an academic interpretation and moved on. I myself am only a quarter Ashkenazi, so no offense taken here. According to them I'm three-quarters man. But where did this loathing come from?

Only a few years later did I learn that hateful places breed hate. On a tour of Auschwitz-Birkenau, this one fat student with mean eyes, cheeks purple with cold, began to scratch the words "Death to left-wingers" onto a wooden wall in the women's camp. An alert teacher intervened and didn't let him finish. His friends consoled him, promising to complete the work when they got back to Israel. They were cloaked with the national flag, wearing yarmulkes, walking among the sheds, filled with hatred—not for the murderers, but for the victims. It was hard to fathom. These kids kept quiet during the heart-to-hearts, but I still got to know them completely, fully, totally.

In the meantime, my career progressed nicely. I was almost a doctor. I had some good recommendations from school principals, had a good handle on death camp floor plans; a loyal, industrious agent of memory. I guided an endless string of tours and rarely came back to Israel. Ruth got used to it, raising our child alone until we were in the black. We were so scared of dropping beneath the poverty line, and these trips filled our bank account.

After proving myself as a guide for high school students, I successfully passed the admissions board to guide military and security forces groups. They were much easier to work with. They showed up in uniform, obedient, never interrupting, listening quietly to my explanations. When I eavesdropped on them, I heard nothing of interest. I missed the kids' subversive chatter. At the beautiful, old synagogue in Tykocin, whose Jews were felled by gunshot in a nearby forest, they put their army berets on their heads and said a prayer for the safety of Israel. *Our Holy Father, stronghold and redeemer of Israel, bless the State of Israel, the source of our redemption*. It was beautiful. I wanted to join in and surrender to Him, but God wasn't there, of that I was sure, and if He was, then He was a shit God, our Shitty Father, a great big shit, and I answered along with them: *Amen*.

At the entrance to the Children's Forest on the outskirts of Tarnow, a man from the military band blew the trumpet in front of three marching rows. That's where the Germans shot ten thousand people, mostly Jews and a few Polish scholars, including eight hundred little children from the Jewish orphanage. I explained to them about how the killing was performed in this place, before organized murders in the camps. It was not pretty. Blood sprayed, bodies twitched, evidence piled up. The contact was too intimate; lots of ammunition was wasted. This served as motivation to build the camps, where the process was more like fumigating for ants or mice, and where Jewish slaves could be used to perform the dirty work. The trumpet player played a pretty, sad tune. A military cantor read the "El Male Rahamim" prayer, they sang the anthem, and female officers placed small teddy bears on the ground, for the children.

These officers had no hatred for the Germans either. In their speeches, the murderers had no image or language. They'd just dropped out of heaven. *We did not come for revenge*, the commanders said in their recurring speeches, standing before silent soldiers in formal uniform, arranged in groups of three.

If you had been serving in the German military at the time, say in the armored corps or in airplane maintenance or in personnel management or in the electronic intelligence bunker, and your beloved homeland was at war with its enemies on all borders, would you have defected if you'd found out that somewhere far off, in the east, people were doing this kind of dirty work? I guess not. I know I wouldn't.

Once, in Birkenau, on an especially hot summer day, after I'd already guided many military delegations, after too much sun and not enough water, I started seeing flashes. I stood in front of the soldiers among the concrete ruins of the death wing, and the questions in the back of my mind punched their way out: "Who among you would have defected?" I blurted.

No hands were raised. Their expressions were embarrassed. The pretty junior officers looked at each other, like, *What does this guy want?*

Then I couldn't resist and asked them another question: "If you knew that one morning you were going to wake up to find out that your eternal, most hated enemies had been wiped off the face of the earth without any blood on your hands and without having to see a single corpse, how many of you would feel sad about it?"

No hands were raised.

The commander of the delegation, a colonel, walked over and whispered in my ear, "They don't understand your question. You're confusing them. What you're doing is inappropriate."

The entire camp was spinning, the treetops, the small buildings, the concrete. *What am I doing. What am I doing.* I didn't mean to lead them to this alley of nightmares. I was sentenced to be here alone.

After dinner at the hotel, during the end-of-day wrap-up talk, I apologized for what I'd said. I explained that I had suffered from heatstroke, I got carried away, I was feeling ambivalent. "I'm a weak person," I told them, and I meant it. I wanted to appease them. I was scared to death to be left without them. I got so carried away with apologizing that finally the commander came over, patted my back, and said, "All right, it's behind us, bygones." As far as I know he never reported the incident.

You might remember that right after I received my doctorate, you summoned me to your pleasant office in that stone building. You said you'd read my dissertation and was impressed, that it was precise, that I'd evaded the curse of sentimentality, that I'd forged an interesting path toward a practical understanding of the annihilation process. You said you'd love to publish my dissertation as a book. That it would require some editing, of course, to make it suitable for a wider audience. I sat before you, proud and grateful. We spoke for quite a while. You asked to hear my opinion on several matters, explaining that you were trying to get some new blood into the field, that there were many subjects just waiting for the right person, but that unfortunately you had no available slots left and could not offer me a full-time job. But, you said, you'd love to use my help on a regular basis for some special tasks, because you were looking for someone just like me, who was able to go deep and had a good familiarity with the territory.

I left your office feeling dizzy. The next day I had to fly back to Poland to guide a group, but I managed to get home in time to go with Ruth to pick up Ido from kindergarten. We sat at a café. I remember every minute of that day. Ruth said: "I've never seen you this happy before."

A few weeks after our meeting you asked me, through one of your department heads, to go visit an archaeological dig at the Sobibor Extermination Camp. You coordinated a visit for me with the Israeli archaeologist who was the head of the dig as part of an international project. He asked for some clarification. No one likes their toes to be stepped on. He wanted to make sure I didn't publish any findings without his explicit permission. I went there the first chance I got, between tours, in a car I rented in Warsaw. I was used to going there by tour bus, with a driver, but this time I drove there myself, and I was enjoying it. East of Lublin, the landscape changed. The villages and farms dwindled, and the fertile meadows were replaced with swamps. All around the ancient forests of Europe thickened, the high treetops darkening the road. I turned right at a sign that said *Sobibor* and drove longer than I remembered from previous visits.

I arrived at a village with single-story homes, chickens and pigs wandering the yards. There wasn't a soul outside, even though it was a weekday. I was almost an hour late to meet the archaeologist, and I'm never late for anything. The road ended at the edge of the village, replaced by a narrow dirt path. This wasn't the road I remembered.

I turned on the GPS, which insisted that I keep going. I stopped the car, got out, and tried to figure out where I was. Suddenly, a door opened, and a man stepped out of a nearby house and into his yard. He had a typical Polish face, tanned from working in the sun, wore wide pants, and looked as if he'd just woken up.

"Sobibor?" I asked.

He said, "Museum?"

His wife stepped outside in a floral dress and stared at me.

It started to rain. The Pole signaled to me to continue down the dirt path. I thanked him and drove on.

The road was bad, full of potholes. If this was the road, then it hadn't been fixed since the war, and it wasn't built for small cars like the one I'd rented. During the Holocaust the Germans closed the roads around the camps, taking a wide berth. Who ever went there by car? Only SS people returning from leave, or reporting to the camp for the first time in their appointment. All the others—the victims—arrived by train. The Ukrainian guards never went anywhere. In their free time, they lit bonfires and got drunk in the woods. This could be the way, I tried to convince myself. Maybe I just couldn't feel the potholes on the bus the way I could now in the car. My phone lost its signal, showing no antennas anywhere around. A fox ran across the road right in front of my car.

Then I crossed a small bridge and finally saw the train tracks. I sighed with relief. The road continued along the tracks for a few hundred meters, and finally I reached the Sobibor train station, which I knew well. A little further after the station, on the other side of the tracks, was the ramp.

I parked the car and opened my umbrella. There was no one around. I walked down the path into the camp, which was nothing like Auschwitz or Majdanek. No barbed wire, no ruins, just the lovely smell of pines in the rain. Everything that happened here is buried deep underground. The Germans had trashed the camp, plowing the earth thoroughly. But my eyes knew where to place the structures in the open space: there was the shed where they were told to remove their clothes, and there was the gate where their heads were shaved. Over there is where people stored the luggage, and this is where the *Himmelstrasse*—the road to heaven—began, where the naked prisoners were urged to run into the gas chambers.

A few Polish workers were standing there now, wrapped in rain ponchos, smoking beside their work tools—shovels, wheelbarrows, and handheld sifters. The archaeologist stood at a distance, bearded and extremely grave. I liked him immediately. I greeted him in Hebrew with relief.

He answered briefly that he was glad to see me, but that they'd been waiting for me in the rain for a long time, and now we had to hurry.

I apologized and described the bad road.

The archaeologist paced in front of me in his work boots and showed me the area that was being uncovered between the trees—a large rectangle, at the bottom of which were the foundations of walls, only a few centimeters high. Judging by their location, the materials, and the laboratory findings, these were the walls of the gas chambers. This finding was startling, especially for people in the field, like us, and clarified the structure of the camp for the first time in history. It was no coincidence you'd sent me there. This used to be the last stop: women and children in one room, men in the other. The door closed, and an engine was started, flowing carbon monoxide into the rooms. I had so many questions, but it was raining harder now, and the Polish workers were impatient, smoking and asking to get into the van that was already waiting for them.

"I'm sorry we don't have more time," said the archaeologist. "But as you can see, they're done for the day. We waited a long time for you. We can continue this over the phone. I'm leaving the country soon, but I'll be back in the spring. It's impossible to work here in winter."

The workers got into the van.

"I'm heading out with them," said the archaeologist. "Are you going to be all right? Do you have a way to get back?"

I thanked him. The van left. I wondered how they could just leave their dig site without any guards, but really, who would come here in the rain? And what was there to steal, anyway?

Now it was just me and the forest and the memory. *I'm singing in the rain!* I felt like dancing all of a sudden, probably because I was gripped with fear. The rain was turning the dirt. I quickened my steps to the car so I could get out of there. I hoped I'd be able to find the road I remembered this time and not have to drive back on that broken road, but that was the only way I found.

I turned on my high beams. The last remains of daylight were barely visible around the treetops. The car was jostled by the potholes. The radio played nothing but static, and I imagined I could hear the Ukrainians singing in the woods, grilling meat and getting drunk, celebrating that day's crop of murders. Soon, an SS car would drive by, a Mercedes or an Opel, stopping me and asking to see my papers, sending me back there. I should have asked the archaeologist to wait for me. It's bad news, being in this forest alone. Only when I reached the paved road again and saw the sign that read *Lublin* did I begin breathing normally again. But I still didn't feel safe. Not at all.

The next day I sent you a brief report of my visit, an initial report is what I called it, and pointed out that there would be more to come. I was on my way to the top.

The Yad Vashem editor proposed we include some photographs. We put quite a bit of work into editing my dissertation, which was very detailed and full of footnotes, into a format more suitable for a wider audience. People love to take a break with some pictures when they read nonfiction, he explained, and they like to see things with their own eyes, to know who they are reading about. There were lots of pictures from the period after the German defeat, when the camps were occupied. Pictures of piles of corpses and of liberated, skeletal prisoners and so on and so forth. But that wasn't what my editor and I had in mind. We wanted pictures taken while the camps were active, and those were hard to find. From Belzec, for instance, where over a period of ten months 500,000 Jews were murdered on their day of arrival, there were a few odd images, which I had spent hours looking at through a magnifying glass and of which I knew every single detail. In one of them, SS man Rudolf Cam is seen in full uniform with crossed arms, his head balding and his eyes blinking at the sun, standing before a row of wooden sheds. Judging by his short, dark shadow, it seems to be early afternoon on a bright day. About ten meters behind him, a woman in a dark dress and a coif—the customary outfit of Orthodox women—is looking straight into the camera. She is wearing clogs, her feet and calves exposed. She does not look scared. Nearby, in the doorway of a shed, is a man in civilian clothing— slacks, a jacket, and a beret—also looking into the camera.

A kind of triangle is formed in this image, but the relationship between the three is unclear, and no one knows whether the Nazi agreed to have the other two included in the picture, though the photographer certainly noticed they were there. Why did he not ask them to move? Why did he choose to commemorate them, too? The matter becomes a bit clearer in another image, taken from the doorway of a wooden shed that housed the Belzec camp staff, showing five figures, probably Jews, arms crossed, well-dressed, as if caught in the midst of a Saturday stroll. These were likely Sonderkommandos on a break, or at least that is the interpretation the picture has gained through the years. It is inconceivable and questionable to me, because they look so relaxed, standing almost languidly before the camera, but it is in line with the testimonies of Sonderkommando survivors from other camps, teaching us that this, to them, had become the world, and they had to serve in it and adjust to its new laws, which were not to be questioned or altered. Still, I hesitated to send these to the editor, and when I did, I pointed out to him that I did not know for certain who the men pictured were, in spite of all my research.

From Majdanek, I sent him some pictures of hard labor: prisoners pushing carts loaded with rocks, their expressions imperceptible in the distance. I also added a few famous images from the Auschwitz Album, taken by SS photographers for unknown purposes, documenting the history of a single transport from Hungary, from the moment they descended the train, through selection and waiting by the gas chambers. I spent hours on end examining these pictures as well, looking through a magnifying glass at the clothing, the paths, the fences, and the faces. Pretty children walking or carried, women wearing coifs and men donning hats. I tried to determine the location and number of SS people and of Jewish slaves awaiting the transport in order to load it onto trucks headed to Kanada Warehouse. I checked how many people were turned left toward labor and how many were turned right toward immediate death. I couldn't get enough of the innocent appearance of the thatch-roofed house where the murders took place, the yard, the windows, and the chimney. One by one, I scanned the faces of the people waiting their turn outside the house on the backdrop of the forest, reading their expressions for clues: did they know what was waiting for them inside or did they believe the lies about showers, food, work? I marked the tiniest details with color and graphics that I labored over on my computer, adding interpretations for each. There are sixty photos in the Auschwitz Album, and I knew each of them by heart, as if I had stood in the very spot where they'd been taken. I chose the most important ones to include in the book.

I was especially mesmerized by photos of the camp staff during free time, like that picture of the SS staff in Sobibor—I knew all of their names—posing casually for the camera, smiling, guns and grenades in their holsters, wearing that elegant Hugo Boss uniform, good-looking people, fine men. Compared to the Sobibor staff, the Belzec staff look like an odd collection of weirdos and psychopaths. Perhaps it is the photographer's fault, or the angle. They are pictured on the backdrop of the camp commander's house, officers in front and soldiers in back, all wearing light-colored coats except for one, in a black coat, recognized as the commander's driver, a bicycle leaning against the wall behind. I know all their names, too.

I hadn't been able to find any significant differences between the resumes and skills of the staff in Sobibor and Belzec, so I have to assume the difference between the photographs has to do with the professionalism of the photographers or their intention of flattering their subjects.

I also sent the editor some rare photos from the Auschwitz satellite camps—Jewish slaves in striped uniforms—and emphasized one image I was especially riveted by, from the Siemens electric component factory near

Auschwitz, showing Jews standing at the assembly line, some of them consulting about some technical issue. If it hadn't been for their shorn heads and the extreme skinniness apparent beneath their stained uniforms, you might think it was just a normal day at work. The slaves are all pictured from behind, their faces unseen, but the German work manager is seen from the front, standing at the end of the hall in suit and tie, talking to one of the men in stripes, hands linked behind his back, as if the Jew were asking him for a raise or time off.

I tried to find out the German's name and what happened to him after the war, but came out empty-handed. He must have climbed up the corporation's career ladder.

I also sent the editor a series of pictures of another kind that had drawn me. They showed the command chain of the Final Solution in official and social gatherings. For instance, Hans Frank, Governor-general of Poland, an attorney by profession, hosting Heinrich Himmler at Wawel Castle in Krakow, the historical seat of Polish kings. Both in uniform, they sit at a table covered with china cups, small liquor glasses, silver spoons, and a trapeze-shaped box—probably chocolates Himmler had brought as a gift. They are enjoying a brief respite together. I also had lots of pictures of Himmler visiting different sites over his empire in a convertible, a small smile on his mousy face. Rumor has it that neither he nor Adolf Hitler liked spending much time at the office. They both preferred to be out in the field, in the open air. I was addicted to these images, from the great leader making speeches to the small man whipping victims on their way to death, because in these images these men looked free and relaxed, comfortable and confident in their skin.

"Thirty Germans, including those who were on vacation, one hundred and fifty Ukrainians, six hundred Jews—that was the staff that carried out the extermination at Treblinka," I explained to my groups. "That was the scale of the operation in other camps, too."

I was prepared for the astounded expressions on their faces. Had the Jews rebelled right away, refusing to cooperate, the operation would not have been carried out so easily, I told them. The Germans would have had to allocate a lot more manpower for the job and things might have been postponed, but no one could say for sure. I read to these students and soldiers the letter sent to Himmler from Odilo Globocnik, who ruled Operation Reinhard camps from Lublin, right after he finished murdering over two million Jews. In the letter, he brags about having completed the task with such small German manpower, and pointed out that some famous industry factories had taken an interest in his efficient work method. I explained the paralyzing fear and the negation of willpower, as well as the fact that the millions of trained Soviet soldiers that had been taken prisoner hardly rebelled. It was the animalistic urge to survive at any cost that kept the machine moving, as well as man's submissiveness in the face of unstoppable power. That was what the German method relied on. "I would have done the same," I told them, "and you probably would have, too. We would have all carried bodies from the gas chambers to the crematorium, pulling gold teeth from their mouths, shearing their hair to feed it into the fire if it meant staying alive one more day, one more hour, one more minute."

We mustn't use the expression "like lambs to the slaughter"—that's what you kept telling us at the guide course. It's equally forbidden at the university. I was always obedient, never using it. But the truth is, we both know that expression is too delicate and merciful: lambs are not killed with poison. They are slaughtered, the flesh and wool spared. The lambs are loved, caressed, fed fresh grass, while the Jews were poisoned with insecticide and rodenticide. I should have told them that, breaking their meaningless melancholy, putting an end to the playing of bland songs on their guitars. The Kaddish, the tears, the candles, all that feel-good nonsense.

I sketched a complete picture of the murderers and their assistants for myself—their customs and agenda, their tools, and the rules within which they operated. But I didn't know the victims. It was impossible in terms of quantity, and was beyond the bounds of my research. Standing before these groups, I listed the names of the countries from which transports arrived at each camp, as well as the number of victims, but I didn't say their names. They were so many, where would I even begin? And they were all treated the same way, like dog food ingredients. I brought the students to the display cases at the Auschwitz Museum, filled with hair, suitcases, prostheses, shoes, and said, "These were people." I wanted them to think about their younger siblings, their parents, their children, and themselves. I couldn't carry that burden myself.

And I succeeded. I was booked for more and more trips, and sometimes stayed out of the country for two months at a time. So I rented a small apartment in Warsaw, near the old ghetto, on a high floor of a large concrete housing project built during the Communist era, the next street over from where Janusz Korczak's orphanage used to be, and where now there is just a regular Polish school. You helped me with the rent check because you appreciated my work and enjoyed its fruits. In the center of the housing project was a large lawn with a jungle gym. I liked to sit on a bench when the weather was nice, watching children and birds and Polish mothers. I invited Ruth to bring Ido and come live with me there several times, just for now, until we got our act together. She didn't say no, but we never executed the plan. I knew this place once swarmed with Jewish life, but it was very hard to see it now. My imagination wasn't strong enough. In the evening, I would watch the lights go on in the buildings across the way. Small families sat down to dinner—mother, father, child, two children, tops. Sometimes no child at all. They barely had children here, as if the lack of Jews had canceled out the need for procreation. I strolled on foot a lot, walking to the old city and along the river, but on very cold winter days I stayed in, listening to music. I liked listening to Bach.

One night I imagined I was a klezmer player in Poland three hundred years ago, playing the violin at weddings, brises, and the celebrations of righteous men, and that I'd heard of some musical genius in Germany, let's say Leipzig, whose music shot up into the heavens, and decided to leave everything behind and travel west to see him. Would he have accepted me as a student, a player, an apprentice? Of course, if I had shown up with yarmulke and fringes he would have refused to have me, that's understandable—I couldn't walk into the church where he worked dressed like that. But what if I'd agreed to dress like a gentile? Would he still have turned me away? In short, I insisted, was Bach an anti-Semite? Did the sight of a Jew, his smell, the way he talked, disgust him? I wanted so badly for the answer to be no. I tried to put the thought out of my mind for a day or two. I went out to guide another tour, and when I returned I listened to the Cello Suites, but my pure pleasure had been hindered. I could no longer listen to the music without obsessing over that question.

Bach and Jews, I typed into the search engine. I found many articles, most of them dealing with the St. John Passion, which Bach had composed for Martin Luther's newly established Protestant church, according to Luther's lyrics. I listened to the piece carefully. A choir of women poured into me, heavenly voices. Then the men appeared, baritones and tenors, a duet in German (I understood most of it), until the women's voices returned to soothe me. Then the tenor sang about the *Juden*, then again about the *Juden* and sweet Jesus, and what the *Juden* had done to him. I could smell the singer's bad breath. I paused the music. It made me feel sick. *Don't go there*, I told my inner klezmer, playing without sheet music, dancing on the bride and groom's table with his torn shoes, among the plates of chopped liver and challah and herring, carried on the aromas of garlic and onion. *He won't take you.*

On the way to Krakow, I introduced them to the Righteous Among the Nations Anna R., an old woman who had remained in her small village her entire life. These days, her grandchildren work her farm with an old tractor and a donkey. I liked her. Her kindness melted my heart, and I think she liked me too. She always seemed happy to see me. On nice days she would come out to meet us in the yard, and on rainy days we would crowd inside her small house. She spoke Polish, and one of her granddaughters translated her words into broken English. Then I told them the story in Hebrew: one night during the war she and her late husband heard a knock on the door. A boy was standing in their doorway, filthy, covered with lice, and starving. Without giving the matter a second thought, they let him in. He told them he'd fled from the Germans and the Polish police, that his hometown had been surrounded, the Jews pillaged, beaten. Those who tried to run were killed, and the others were taken by train to an unknown destination. The boy's entire family was put on the train, while he'd managed to run to the woods and survive for a few weeks eating food he'd stolen from farms. By the time he came knocking on their door he was prepared to die of hunger, cold, and grief.

Anna took pity on him, bathing him, feeding him, and washing his clothes. He spent that night in their home, and when he awakened the next day they asked him to leave, fearing for themselves and for their children. "But the sun shone," she said, always smiling when she reached this part, "and the boy decided he wanted to live and begged to stay. I wanted to send him away," Anna confessed. "I knew what the Germans were capable of, but my husband said, 'We've got no choice, we've got to let him stay.'" She agreed.

They set up a hiding place for him in the barn, tasking their eldest daughter, who was twelve years old at the time, with serving his meals. Sometimes, under cover of dark, they invited him into their home to dine with them or warm himself at the fireplace. Her face lit up when she described it. A few months later, they heard the Germans had burned down the house of a family who had harbored Jews in a nearby village. Hearing this, the boy said he would return to the woods, though they didn't ask him to. But they remained in touch with him. Twice a week they would hide food and clothes for him in a secret spot on the outskirts of the forest. "Srulik," Anna said in conclusion, putting her hands together, "that was his name, and he lived, he lived, he stayed alive!"

"Applaud her," I commanded them, "applause, right now, as loud as you can."

"Who among you would have rescued a strange, filthy boy who knocked on your door at night, putting your own life and the lives of your children at risk?" I asked them in our nightly session at the hotel.

Silence. Then whispering. Their brains ground through the options. How to get out of this?

"He isn't one of your people," I reminded them. "He's of a different faith. You don't even know him. You have no obligation toward him, other than being humans."

A few raised their hands.

"Would you die for him?" I persisted. "Would you risk having your home set on fire with you and your children inside?"

At this point the hands usually came down.

"There are no specific characteristics that define the Righteous Among the Nations," I told them. "You'll find hardly any famous, successful, genius, or exceptionally intellectual people on the list. Most of them were just regular people, like Miss Anna, whom we visited today. I have no idea how many books she's read in her lifetime. She didn't attend high school, that's for sure. She spent her entire life working in the field and on tending to the pigs on her farm and raising children. But she has a good heart. She took him in. There were plenty of other people—murderers, cowards, who burned Jews alive, who turned them in, but there were also people like her.

"I ask myself," I told them, "what would I have done in her place? I don't know. I would probably be too afraid to take the risk, and it's killing me, it won't let me go, because that's the only question we can ask ourselves as human beings."

The teachers fidgeted uncomfortably in the first row.

With time, I took less care with my words. The dilemma raced across the children's faces. Common sense intervened. They had been taught to use certain criteria—they oughtn't open the door to just anyone, it depended who the person was and where they had come from. They would check carefully, in the meantime closing the door in the person's face. The more philosophical of the group would have rescued no one. Only the modest, the simple, the kind, would. I am not one of them, I told myself, and it made it difficult for me to carry on the conversation. I cannot even manage to love these children, who are my people and have done nothing wrong. I attribute them with malice based merely on their expressions and bits of dialogue. How would I ever take a strange boy in?

In Treblinka I explained, against the backdrop of forest birdsong, that this camp had no labor component, only extermination. Each time a transport arrived, the famously simple process began: passengers disembarked, stunned, urged on with beatings and shouting, ordered to put down their things and undress quickly. The naked women's hair was cut off before they were led down a narrow path to the bathrooms. Signs in Germans pointed the way, and those who dawdled were whipped, but rather than a bathroom, the Germans pushed them into the gas chamber. Thirty minutes later, Jewish slaves removed twisted, bloated bodies from the room, wrapped around each other. They pulled gold teeth from the corpses' mouths and tossed the bodies into pits. Every few days the piles would be set on fire under the open sky.

Sometimes I got into the details of each step in the process, more than necessary, until the teachers or the commanders signaled to me that time was running out and that we had to move on. Then I would shake myself and say, "All right, let's keep going," and wonder why I behaved the way I did. For instance, I told them more than they needed to know about the haircutting process; how the Germans whipped the naked women into the haircutting room, ordered them to sit on stools. The Jewish barbers stood behind them, ordered to use only five clips for each woman in order to save time. The women's heads bled with the violence of this urgent cutting, while all around

Germans and Ukrainians whipped both the women and the barbers, urging them on. The barbers tossed the hair into suitcases on the floor, lest it be trampled. Each haircut lasted only a few seconds, after which the Jewish women were rushed to the path leading to the gas chambers. The young women in my groups were always astounded, their glossy, healthy hair flowing. I paused. How these stories riveted my twisted soul! I allowed the forest to sound its rustles, glanced at the pale sky over their heads, at the treetops, afraid to meet their eyes. "Come," I said, and they followed me through a field of stones, wrapped in their flags.

Back on the bus, one of the teachers sat next to me. She had short hair and a small, doubtful smile. Ever since Eliezer the survivor had broken his hip, and Yohanan had collapsed in Auschwitz and was no longer able to take his place, I mostly sat alone on the bus.

"Thank you for your fascinating explanation," she said. "You seem to be living those events."

I told her I was trying my hardest, that sometimes I got carried away, and that I hoped I did all right.

"No, you were terrific, this entire tour," she said. "Now, and back at the hotel when you talked about the Righteous Among the Nations. I can tell you really take this to heart."

We were riding down the highway. Behind us phones beeped along to the soundtrack of *Schindler's List*, which was being shown on the bus's screens.

"It must be very difficult," she said, then waited for me to respond.

I tried to assess her age. She might have been forty, even fifty, but no older than that. She was wearing a diamond wedding ring. She could have been my older sister, but not my mother. I was aching to speak to someone. During that time, the burden was accumulating. But her smile bothered me. It didn't seem decent.

"I think you have to have more faith in the children," she said. "They can tell when someone doubts them. It hurts. The most important thing for a child is to know they are trusted."

"You're right," I told her. "I'm trying."

"They're excellent children," the teacher said. By this point she was getting agitated. "In a few months' time they'll go to the military and we'll be trusting them with our lives. They will be risking their own lives for ours. We have to have faith in them."

"I'm sure they'll make good soldiers," I said.

My answer made her furious. "They'll make more than just good soldiers." She said, raising he voice a little. "They're good people. Wise. Healthy. That's how they should be treated. With love. They are our hope and our future."

I didn't argue.

"Look into their eyes," she proposed, and put her cold hand on mine in a gesture of mercy. "That's what I do. That's how I connect to them."

"Yes, yes, I'll try, I'll try harder. I want to love them, to connect to them, to not fear them. Truly, I do."

I took a group from a yeshiva high school to Rabbi Moses Isserles's synagogue in Kazimierz. It used to be the Jewish quarter of Krakow and is now full of nostalgia, demonstrated through restaurants featuring live performances from Polish klezmers, Judaica and holy book stores. This artificial longing used to move me, but after a few visits I grew tired of it. The real Jews, the ones who wanted to live, who haggled, who spoke Yiddish, who breathed air through their nostrils and exhaled it here on their streets, were not loved. I was glad to see these students with their yarmulkes wandering around here among the pillaged buildings. I felt a hankering to hear a prayer and hoped they would awaken the old synagogue to life. I couldn't bear the Jewish backdrop of this town any longer.

They granted my wish, praying and singing, and I joined them for the bits I knew. For a moment, I felt uplifted. We walked out to the cemetery adjacent to the synagogue and I led them to Isserles's grave. They were moved by it. The school principal spoke of Isserles's greatness as a rabbinical judge and an adjudicator. I couldn't tell you one thing Isserles did to promote humankind, but I kept my mouth shut.

There were no women in the group, and perhaps that's why these students were quieter and more serious than other school kids. They said the Kaddish prayer in the rain. I showed them the nearby grave of Shmuel Bar Meshulam, who was the physician of the ancient kings of Poland and had come to Krakow from Milan with the entourage of Princess Bona Sforza, who married Sigismund I the Old, King of Poland, and lived with him at Wawel Castle. She only agreed to be examined by the Jewish doctor she'd brought with her from Italy. I took them to see a few other synagogues in the quarter. That was their request—to move among the shadows of Jews.

I listened to them singing and praying in the empty synagogues, closed my eyes, and swayed like them with devotion, trying to get carried away with them. But nothing rose from within my soul, and the image of God before my eyes resembled a tattered merchant who has gone bankrupt, his glasses sliding off his nose as he tries in vain to put order in the accounting ledgers strewn over his desk.

The next day, as we finished our visit to Auschwitz and were leaving the camp, they waved the Israeli flag, sang "Am Yisrael Chai" at the tops of their lungs, and danced with a decorated Torah Ark they passed from one person to the next. I walked over to their principal in a brief moment of respite and whispered, "This is where our people are buried, it isn't right to dance."

"We're alive," said the principal. "And our Torah lives. We have returned to our homeland, and therefore we dance in celebration of the grace of God. In the end, we won. You can argue with me about it for the rest of your life, it'll be no good, my friend. This is what we believe. There is no room for despair. We are the future and the hope. Join us, come dance." Thus said the yeshiva principal before he returned to the wild circle.

I returned to Israel urgently, having been summoned by Ruth. Ido was refusing to go back to kindergarten. Some boys were bullying him. He'd stayed home for almost a week. Ruth consulted with the teacher, but it was no good. The boys always managed to catch him in some remote corner and beat him up. The teacher spoke to them and spoke to them before finally giving up. I got on a flight as soon as the tour was over and arrived early in the morning, just as he woke up to go to school.

Ruth was trying to get him dressed, and he just stood there, his eyes extinguished, limp and humiliated. It was awful to see my child looking like this. I had brought him a small gift from Warsaw, but he had no reaction. "I'll go to kindergarten with you today and I'll take care of it," I promised.

He got dressed with heavy movements and terrible helplessness. He wasn't especially short or weak, but he couldn't hit back, and these boys took advantage of that. I knew this because I used to be like him, but I had since realized: to gain any kind of social standing, man must be capable of killing.

The teacher was surprised to see me—I was a rare vision. "Daddy came with you, how fun," she told Ido, who was gripping my arm, his eyes on the floor, and wouldn't let go.

"Can I speak to you in private," I said.

She said this wasn't a convenient time, all the kids were just coming in and she had to greet them.

"We have to," I insisted. "He's being beaten. He doesn't want to come here." I was very tired from the flight, and morning ruckus ensued all around. I saw enemies in all the boys' eyes, and accomplices in the girls'. We were standing on the sidelines while the teacher busied herself with other children. I asked Ido to point out which kids had been hitting him. He signaled for me to duck down, whispered three names into my ear, and pointed them out. They were cheerful just like any other normal kids that morning, and their conscience didn't seem to weigh on them at all. One of them had just said goodbye to his mother, so I walked over to talk to her. I asked her if she knew her son was hitting mine.

"What's going on here?" she asked, baffled. "Since when do we talk this way around the children?" She turned to the teacher for help.

"Please," said the teacher, "let me handle it. Not like this."

Kindergarten was hostile territory, a ring of abuse. Ido showed me the hidden corner behind the mattresses where the kids had grabbed him and stepped on him, as well as the spot in the yard where they had hit him over the head and forced him to eat sand. I towered over that one boy, who finally looked scared, and shouted, "Don't you dare touch my son!"

His mother screamed, puffing up like a wild turkey, but I didn't care. The entire kindergarten railed around me. I didn't know these parents, but now they knew me. I stayed with Ido for a long time, until things calmed down and he agreed to say goodbye. Force is the only way to resist force, and one must be prepared to kill.

Ruth waited for me at home. "I fixed it," I told her when I got back. "They won't lay a finger on him again."

I took advantage of my brief stay in Israel to meet some survivors. I'd been searching for them everywhere, their absence standing out during the trips. I had a shortlist of potential candidates I'd received from you, and with help from your guidance department I called them to schedule some meetings. It turned out one of them had passed away. A child's voice told me over the phone that his grandpa was dead and he'd received his old phone. I apologized. Of the others, I'd managed to schedule an immediate meeting with only one, who lived in Tel Aviv and sounded alert and eager to talk.

When I arrived at the meeting, I was greeted by a tan, fit old man, well-dressed, a small lapdog at his feet. Wow, this seemed promising. A good-looking woman came to say a polite hello before disappearing into one of the rooms. The apartment was pleasant and sunlit. I took a seat across from him and waited to hear his story.

"So you're from Yad Vashem," he said. "That's right," I confirmed.

"Funny to meet like this again," he said, a hint of European accent in his voice. "I don't remember meeting you before," I told him.

"Not you, your predecessor," he clarified. "Over fifty years ago. I was a young man back then. After meeting him, and a few other unpleasant events, I left the country. I only came back a few months ago. I got remarried and my wife wanted to live in Israel. I don't think you can hurt me anymore. That's why I called and suggested we talk. I wanted to meet you again very much."

Why would we hurt this man? I wondered, waiting for his story. I began to introduce myself and the purpose of my visit, but, accustomed to giving orders, he signaled to me impatiently that there was no need. His young, healthy appearance was misleading. His eyes were full of ancient hostility.

"I had a fine life here in Israel. I had two children and had managed to get over what happened there. Until, one day, people pointed at me on the street. I was going to lunch, and they said I was a kapo. A criminal. Then the police took me in for questioning. And you helped them. People heard about it. You put it in the newspaper. I had to leave the country. I spent an entire lifetime in exile because of you. I thought you came here today to apologize, but I see no apology in your eyes."

I told him that was an unfortunate story, but that I wasn't familiar with the facts.

"The facts are," he blurted, "that I was twenty years old

and taken to dig tunnels in Gross-Rosen. We dug with our hands. They appointed me head of my shed because I was strong and never broke. All around me people died off like flies. They spent a month or two in the tunnels before they kicked the bucket, but in our shed things were a little better, because we had discipline and worked hard, and therefore got a little more food. Another quarter of potato per day could save a man. We were always on time to start work right at dawn and stood up straight during roll call, never giving them any reason to beat us, though it still happened on occasion. There were a few lazy people who created some problems, didn't want to wake up in the morning, didn't want to work, and were putting us all in danger. All I wanted was to buy us some time, get us a little more food, one day at a time, until it was over. I didn't exactly have an easy go of it, either. They murdered my entire family. By the time they released us I weighed thirty-five kilos, half of what I weigh today. But I held on. I had to be harsh with the men who broke discipline, risking the rest of us. I had to beat them and give them less food. This wasn't Switzerland, sir, it was hell. I'm sorry, but I survived because I was strong. It was thanks to my strength that I went back to living, eating, sleeping with women, going to the movies, making money. Doing everything free men do. And then these people point at me on the street. You reported me to the police, saying I was a bad kapo; that I collaborated with the Germans. Tell me, was there a single Jew who didn't collaborate? The Judenrat? The snitches? All those Sonderkommandos? Did they not collaborate? Why don't you do anything to them? All I did was take responsibility. I could have decided to worry only about myself and my little piece of bread. Instead, do you have any idea how many lives I saved?" He poured himself water with a trembling hand. His wife came out of one of the inner rooms.

It would be interesting to take a look at his file, I thought. I had to say something, it was the humane thing to do. "We see things differently these days," I said, and could carry on no longer. His eyes were pleading. He was waiting for me to offer forgiveness, but I couldn't. I didn't know the facts. He may have suffered an injustice or he may have not. "Would you agree to speak to high school students?" I asked. "Would you be willing to tell them your story?"

He shook his head no. All his energy had drained out. Tears were in his eyes. The mask of youth had disintegrated.

"You're cruel," his wife told me, pointing me out the door.

That night, Ruth got Ido to speak. He confessed that ever since the visit I had paid to his kindergarten no one had hit him, but no one was willing to play with him, either.

I thought about the robust man I'd met that morning, who'd survived thanks to his strength, and then I thought about Ido, who couldn't hit back.

He asked that I take him to kindergarten again the next day and stay there with him. I explained that I had to go back to my job, abroad, that people were waiting for me there.

"What's your job, Dad?" he asked.

"He tells them about what happened," Ruth offered.

"What happened?" Ido widened his eyes with worry.

"There was a monster that killed people," I said.

"And you fight the monster?" he asked, excited.

"It's already dead," I tried to explain. "It's a memory monster."

Following my meeting with the survivor, I came up with the idea of creating an organized list of kapos. I even wrote you a memo about it, and at nights, in the hotel, I prepared an initial characterization of a computerized resource, including pictures. Most of the information already exists, but it's scattered all over the place. Throughout the years, there has been an aversion to centralizing the information due to foreign and emotional considerations that are of no interest to a historian. I wrote to you that we would have to make some principle decisions regarding the definition of what makes a kapo, but without splitting hairs. A kapo is a kapo. For the sake of caution, we would need verification from several sources, and if evidence was lacking, the survivor would enjoy the benefit of the doubt.

"What do we need this for?" you asked in your response.

I said, "So we may know the truth; so we may enhance the difference between black and white."

"There is no black and white in history," you said, writing me off.

Your response seemed rash to me, but I decided to let it go. I didn't want to anger you. As it turned out, my restraint was wise. Just a few days later, your head of computerization contacted me as per your recommendation, requesting my assistance with a death camp visualization project. He explained you'd been contacted by a company that develops virtual reality products and offered a collaboration, and that since Yad Vashem was seeking ways to reach a younger audience, you agreed.

"It's a game," I told your computer guy.

He protested. "What are you talking about? It isn't a game, it's a visualization. It's educational."

Yad Vashem wanted me to help the company with some problems that had come up during the development stage. Reverently, I asked if this was a volunteer job, and your guy said I should agree on a fee directly with the start-up company.

I wrote to them from Poland, and they offered a fraction of their shares in return. One day, they might be worth a lot of money. I think it was a quarter-percent of a share.

I agreed. I even boasted to Ruth about having received shares from a technology company. They paid for my flight, and in the brief respite between tour groups I visited their offices, in some new business district on the edge of Tel Aviv.

I sat down with a young guy who showed me what they'd accomplished so far. The work was very raw. It included an "Arbeit Macht Frei" sign and some sheds, as well as a crematorium chimney. He apologized that the graphics weren't complete yet and said they would be improved. But it wasn't Auschwitz, nor any other camp I knew, and he said that was exactly why they wanted my advice. They wanted it to look as real and authentic as possible.

I spent a few good hours with him, going over the details one by one: the gate and the guard towers and the train tracks and the color of the dirt and the shape of the ramp and the manner in which the paths split right and left, the wood from which the sheds were built, and the electric connections on the fences. They had made plenty of mistakes.

A few weeks later, he sent me a visualization of the undressing room and the gas chambers. I gave lots of notes. We were far from being finished. For instance, they were wrong about the spot from which the can of poison was tossed in, and they didn't know there was an elevator that carried the bodies from the doorway to the gas chamber up to the crematoriums. And they had missed the teeth examination part, and didn't understand how the crematoriums had been loaded at all. So many mistakes.

"What are you going to do with this?" I asked him the next time we met.

He stared at me, pretending not to understand. "It's a collaboration with Yad Vashem," he said.

I persisted: "I know that, but what are you going to do with it? And where are the people? The victims?"

He said that would be handled during the next phase. The intention was to provide the experience of a prisoner ("a victim," I corrected) as well as a guard ("a murderer," I corrected again). He asked me about the sensations of prisoners and guards (I didn't bother to correct him again). What could I tell them about their psychology?

I was deterred by the question. I told him I was an expert on extermination, not the mind. "Oh, I see," he said.

I visited the company offices a few times and enjoyed being there. There was a creative atmosphere: young men in T-shirts sitting in front of large screens, walking around, eating bananas, drinking espresso from a machine. I saw one of them working on a visualization of the Colosseum. A man was eaten by a lion and the crowd roared. Another guy was working on a game where players trapped slaves in the African jungle. The players burned down the village and threw down nets to capture males and fertile females. I figured them out.

"It's going to be a game," I told my guy, the one in charge of the camps.

Finally, he conceded, "You can call it that if you want. People love horror games." I have no idea why he admitted it.

I tried to change my attitude and be more empathetic. The next time I guided a tour group, I tried my best to memorize the names of all the children and teachers, committing their faces to memory. I showed no chagrin when they wrapped themselves in flags and sang. I even sang along with them. I listened patiently to their recitation, trying to find merit in each piece of reading.

We were standing on the edge of the Chelmno forest, where the gas trucks came and where the dead were buried.

"My grandmother's parents died here," one girl said shyly. "They were from Lodz."

I held on to her personal story and asked her to tell us everything she knew. She was charming and smart and told the story well—what she knew of it, at least, which wasn't much. I asked how her grandmother had survived, and she hesitated before saying she wasn't sure. Her grandmother didn't like to talk about it. She was just a kid.

I pushed her. I told her the Germans first sent over twenty thousand children on a special roundup. Their parents dressed them as warmly as possible, as if they were going on a field trip. There are photos of the children waiting to be picked up. The parents were told their children were being sent to a special children's colony, and they never returned.

The girl didn't know what to say. She said she had no way of finding out, because her grandmother was dead.

For some reason, her ignorance upset me. I signaled to the students to stop singing and began my explanations. I told them that in this space, between the village and the forest, the Germans performed a pilot run of their poison extermination. Eichmann visited when they started using gas trucks, dropping in to see how things worked, even before the Wannsee Conference. He saw the entire extermination process with his own eyes, from the arrival at the village castle through loading onto trucks, killing, the unloading of bodies, the pulling of gold teeth, and the tossing into pits. When he was put on trial in Jerusalem, he said it was hard to watch, but that he'd learned some important lessons to be used in other camps, where the idea of trucks was rejected in favor of immobile facilities.

"Can you tell us something else about the children?" a teacher asked. I said I didn't know what I could tell them other than the horror.

"Do we know their names?" she insisted.

I told her some of them were known, but most of them were not.

"That's terrible," the teacher cried. "Just to think about them arriving here without their parents, in these trucks. How can you explain such cruelty?"

I spread my arms and said human beings were capable of anything, especially murder. They relied on ideology or religion. In recent centuries nationalism has served as a good excuse, but mostly people liked seeing other people's children dying. Even us Jews, back in biblical times, murdered women and children, I reminded them, by explicit orders from God. I don't know why I decided to get into that, it was clearly a mistake.

"How dare you make that comparison?" the teacher railed, taking one step forward, prepared to defend our national honor.

I told her I wasn't making any comparison, it's just that children have always been killed, even now.

"Not like that," she said.

"That's true," I said, "but your question is feigning innocence. Don't you know people are murderers? It's in our nature."

When we walked back to the bus, they talked about me behind my back. There was no more affection between us.

After that trip, I received a notification from the travel agency that arranged the administrative aspect of the trips and paid my dues that the customers had not been satisfied. Though my knowledge and professionalism were perfect, as the manager who spoke to me said, the client was unhappy with my emotional content and overall message. They claimed I made no connection with the children and made them feel despair, going so far as to hurt the honor of the victims.

I wrote a furious letter to the travel agency, explaining that this was, at best, a terrible misunderstanding, and, at worst, a lie. I clarified the facts, but also promised to take the criticism to heart and try to do better. Sometimes the educational message and historical facts clash—that was my way of explaining it away—and I would try to buff down that friction.

My explanation was accepted, and the manager called me back, speaking in an appeased tone, saying I was one of their best guides, there was no doubt about that. They had received excellent reviews about me in the past, and of course meant no offense, it's just that it's always best to learn from criticism.

"Of course," I said, and that was that.

The guide for most VIP tours of the camps was usually the press attaché from the Israeli embassy—a Polish Jew who had migrated to Israel, then returned to live in Poland. I'd met him once or twice while I stayed there. One night, the consul called me urgently and asked if I happened to be free the following day to guide the Minister of Transportation, because the regular guide had been involved in a car accident and was lightly injured, and I came highly recommended by Yad Vashem. I happened to be free. I'd been intending to work on proofreading the book, but I was happy to put it off for this opportunity. The Minister of Transportation was in Poland on an official visit and wanted to visit one of the sites of the Holocaust. Since he'd already visited Auschwitz a few years ago as part of the March of the Living, he wanted to visit Treblinka this time.

I looked for a new outfit. I never thought too much about what I wore for normal tours, but I had to dress up nice for the minister. The shops around the ghetto were already closed, but I knew the big mall was open late. I called Ruth from the taxi, told her about the invitation, and asked her what she thought I should wear. She was too preoccupied to think about that. She told me Ido had come home from kindergarten with a scratch on his forehead. He'd been pushed and was refusing to go back again.

"Listen," I told her, I might have been gruff. "I have an important day tomorrow; I'm guiding the minister. I'll deal with the kindergarten stuff when I get back to Israel." I was angry with her and the child. I wanted him to get over it already; to hit back.

I got to the mall in time to buy a button-down and some slacks at an international brand-name store.

I knew Treblinka like the back of my hand. I didn't need any special preparation. I only warned myself to behave, to be informative, interesting, and awe-inspiring. Not to be dragged into any statements that were too original. I could do it. It was my job. I was the best of my kind.

The next morning, I was picked up in a large car. The ambassador was sitting inside. We were briefly introduced. I tried not to get too excited, but it was definitely a step up. I decided not to spare my honor and added the title "doctor" to my name, and the ambassador mentioned again that the consul had received a warm recommendation of me from Yad Vashem. "The minister likes to keep things short," said the ambassador. "The entire visit is planned to last no longer than thirty minutes. It's cold today. It's symbolic, no need to linger over every single detail."

I nodded and made the appropriate adjustments.

We waited for the minister to come out of the hotel with his entourage. He was accompanied by some aides and security guards. I recognized his face from television and was truly excited when he got in the car. I almost took a bow when we were introduced. He asked my name, where in Israel I was from, and how many years I'd been doing this job, and that was the end of our chit-chat. Most of the way he was busy talking on the phone with Israel about some urgent matter under his jurisdiction that had made the news and consulting with his media advisor, who was sitting beside him.

The ambassador and I sat silently, staring at the frozen ground outside. It was nice and warm in the car. The police car rode ahead of us with flashing lights, making way for us through traffic. The ambassador and his advisor formulated a response to something together. We arrived at the familiar turn to Treblinka, near the train tracks, and turned onto the inner road leading to the camp. The trees were naked, the wind was chilling, and snow began to fall.

I cleared my throat and waited for the minister to step out of the car. "Between July 1942 and August 1943 more than 800,000 Jews were murdered in this place, almost all on the day they arrived," I began.

The minister placed a yarmulke on his head and took large, quick steps ahead, as if he were there to take over the place. His guards and aides rushed all around him. I continued my explanations. The minister nodded, not listening.

"Where's the photographer?" the media advisor asked, panicked, and gesticulated to urge him to the head of the line, to document the visit.

We walked through the field of stones commemorating the exterminated communities and reached the monument, where I managed to get a few words out while the minister placed a wreath on the monument. He didn't look at me or ask any questions. The photographer documented him from all angles, standing in front of the monument with his head lowered, until finally the minister said, "Okay, guys, let's get out of here." It really was very cold.

Back in the car, I asked the ambassador's deputy in a whisper if that was all right, and he said it was excellent, exactly what it should have been. "You were great," he emphasized.

Indeed, I was invited a few more times to accompany important people—not the highest-ranking ones, not ministers, but senior servants and vice-ministers and the like, even after the regular embassy guide returned to work.

On the first free day I had after that, I returned to Sobibor to dig. Really dig, with a hoe, and with my hands, on my knees, mining for bits of bone, collecting pins and buttons left behind by the dead. The archaeologist didn't ask any unnecessary questions. He'd agreed for me to come as soon as I'd called him.

I left Warsaw at dawn—I couldn't sleep anyway—and arrived around noon. I'd lost cell service in the forest again, and even the car radio had stopped playing, but I found the way more easily this time.

The archaeologist added me to the group of Polish laborers, who didn't seem pleased about it. I tried to tell them I was only there for a few hours. I didn't want them to think I was there to steal their jobs. But my Polish was horrendous. I'd never made a real effort to learn the language properly, and they didn't understand. They dug a new hole, first beating the ground hard, then, once the soft layer beneath was exposed, switching to small pickaxes. The archaeologist took samples of the soft dirt to be tested in a lab. The new hole was close to the spot where the walls of gas chambers had been uncovered. Other holes in the area had revealed remains of bones, rusty spoons, hair pins, and other personal effects.

My hands began to hurt pretty quickly, but I didn't allow myself to take any breaks, even when the Poles stopped to eat and rest. The archaeologist offered me a part of his sandwich and I took a quick bite standing up because the ground was so cold. He told me that in a few days he would be going to Israel to celebrate one of his three sons' bar mitzvahs. I heard a bus approaching and pulling up. When the people descended I recognized Hebrew, which sounded foreign and out of place. Their guide explained that this path was where the Jews were whipped and rushed toward the gas chambers. I took another bite of the sandwich and kneeled inside the pit again. Now I dug with my hands, no gloves, seeking hard contact. My hands were scratched, my back hurt, and the Poles used their lunch break to its fullest degree, standing around, smoking and watching me dig.

The tour group came nearer and was standing almost over my head at this point. The guide explained the digs taking place on the premises. I lowered my head and waited for them to leave with their guide and his explanations.

"Look at how they dig, these derelicts," one of them said. "With their hands. I have an aunt who was murdered here. I hope he isn't touching her with his filthy hands."

I had to hold back not to step out of the hole and come at him. I was furious.

"The chamber was connected to the motor of an old tank and the people inside were poisoned with carbon monoxide," the guide continued, using phrases that glorified the process. I heard myself in his voice and was appalled. He had no mercy. I recalled how much appreciation I had for the undertaker who had crawled into my father's grave to receive the shrouded body, taking him in his arms and placing him tenderly on the ground. I realized that's what I was trying to do down in that pit. I was about to lose hope of finding anything down there, but as evening descended my fingers bumped into something hard. I grabbed hold of it before I lost it. "I found something," I declared, and pulled out a key, corroded at the tip but retaining its shape.

The archaeologist came closer, took the key from my hands, and said, "Nice work. We don't find this kind of thing just every day."

He took down the date and time of the find, the location of the pit. He took a photo of the key, slipped it into a small bag, and sealed it.

"Let me look at it for a moment," I asked. I looked at the key from every angle, searching for a hint or a mark so that I wouldn't have to try every door in Europe in search of the appropriate lock. I returned the key.

Suddenly, the archaeologist smiled at me, lighting up the forest for a moment. I liked his tough face and strong arms. Perhaps the two of us together would have been able to kill one German man. Not with the children. Not with the women. Not when we were starving. Not facing the barrels of rifles. It would be arrogant to think that could be possible.

The workers were eager to get out of there, but I thought about sticking around a little longer until it grew completely dark.

"Don't stay here alone," the archaeologist said, reading my mind. "This is a job. We finish and we leave. Otherwise we lose our minds. It's too awful."

Another question arrived from the editor: why did I need such a long, practically glorifying description of Reinhard Heydrich, which did not directly contribute to the subject of my research—the matter of unity and difference in the extermination mechanism in Final Solution camps?

I had a clear answer to that and was surprised an editor employed by you would even ask such a thing. Let's put aside the fact that Heydrich was the operations officer of the Final Solution and the originator of the Wannsee Conference. Isn't it enough that Operation

Reinhard, which utilized the camps in Treblinka, Belzec, and Sobibor, and which the book depicts at length, was named after him?

This was my answer to the editor, but he wouldn't let go. Why, then, he persisted, was there a need to describe the beauty of the murderer and his fine manners, which had captivated the Führer's heart; his athletic abilities, and the fact that he had been a fighter pilot during the offensive on the Russian front, along with an official image of him in SS uniform? And why was it important to point out his courage in riding alone with his driver in a Mercedes with the roof lowered, allowing fighters of the Czech underground to assassinate him, and his slow death after a bit of fabric made of horsehair penetrated the gunshot wound in his belly, creating septicemia that caused his death? The editor marked whole paragraphs to be slated for cutting.

He's got a point, I thought. He was right. I was looking for heroes to connect the events, and finding them on the German side. Loathsome heroes, but heroes nonetheless. Had they completed their mission and won the war, humanity would have exalted them, building monuments in their honor, naming garden cities in the east, stadiums, and concert halls after them. No one would have been digging through sites of human waste in the forests, which would be forever erased from our memories.

To test my hypothesis, and before answering the editor again, I decided to run an experiment. I presented the next youth group I'd guided with a picture of Heydrich at his prime, in official uniform. I Photoshopped his swastikas off but left the other decorations and badges. I didn't tell them who the man in the picture was, and asked that if one of them happened to recognize him, to keep it to themselves. I asked the kids what they thought of this man.

"Serious," said one girl. "Level-headed," said another. "Hot," someone giggled in the back. "A man who knows what he wants," said a boy. "A man with a vision." "Strong."

The experiment's results were clear. That's why we'd forgiven them so quickly, and that is the danger in the memory virus we injected into these children's bodies. I had it too. I demanded that the editor leave the chapter untouched. I told him it was important.

The project manager at the gaming company informed me that they had completed the Auschwitz facilities and were about to begin designing the human figures. *We've defined three groups*, he wrote to me, *Germans, Jewish slaves, and Jews that were sent immediately to the gas chambers*. He asked if they had gotten the distribution correctly. I wrote to him that there were other subgroups, such as kapos, Sonderkommandos, German criminal prisoners, gypsies, Ukrainian guards, doctors, and victims of experiments. The Germans also had a myriad of roles, from accounting clerk to head of extermination rooms. He wrote back right away and asked that I detail the characteristics of every group in terms of activities, daily schedules, appearance, and, as much as possible, their state of mind.

I was impressed by his thoroughness and his desire to achieve a perfect result. *This is how these people get rich*, I thought, and I was glad to be a part of it. He sent me samples of the figures he'd already designed, but they were faceless. He explained that the faces would be added later, using real photos of Nazis and Jews.

In a dream I jotted down as soon as I woke up in the darkness of a Poland dawn, I was walking out of a jewelry store on a sunless street, having looked for a gift for Ruth to appease her for my lengthy absence. I was approached by a Jew with a top hat, beard, and polite eyes, who asked me to join a minyan. Normally I refused such offers, but this time I wanted to do it.

"Where?" I asked.

He pointed to a nearby door.

"There's a synagogue there?" I asked, surprised. I thought I knew all the synagogues in this city.

"It's just a small place," he said. "We only took over a little while ago. We did some renovations. It's a synagogue for tailors, cobblers, simple people."

He led me into a small room with a low ceiling, one row of benches along the walls, just like in a gym locker room, shoes and socks beneath them. There were a few men in there, in different stages of undressing, as well as one woman in a bra with a small child, whom she protected as I walked in.

"What's she doing here?" I asked, running my eyes over the room in search of a holy arc and prayer books. "I don't have a yarmulke," I told the man.

"No matter," he said, "we're not strict. Let's turn toward the east and begin." Then he raised his voice and said, "Bless the Lord."

One or two replied with a meek mumble.

He was unsatisfied, and signaled to me to answer him. "Bless the Lord, blessed be He forever," I said.

The others all stood around in their underwear; only my guide and I were dressed. The woman tried to conceal her nudity, and the child was clearly cold. The man continued reading out the blessings, reaching Shema Israel, which made my heart tremble. His public was not participating, and my host prayed alone. I saw his body moving. His speech became too fast, it was no longer praying, but a flow of mumbling, a clear combination of words sounded only every once in a while, *gather in your grain, new wine, and olive oil.*

He's reading too quickly, I thought. *That's no way to pray to God.* Suddenly he signaled to me to get out, quickly.

"But wait," I said, "what about all these people?" I ran after him, because the large iron door was beginning to close.

We were both in a dark interior yard. "What's going to happen to them? What about the others?" I asked.

"They'll manage," he said. "They have their hiding places. Shake your clothes, hard," he said, and began to speak the Kaddish prayer.

I arrived for a short break in Israel, having determined to move on to the next chapter of my life. I would complete my obligations in Europe but would not take on new ones, and would use the time to look for a teaching position, even an adjunct position at one of the universities, or—if need be—at a high school.

I informed Ruth of my plans and she was glad. Ido was thrilled to have me home. He was in the middle of his summer break and we spent a wonderful week together, attached at the hip. Ruth said she'd never seen him that happy before. I spent evenings proofreading the book that was about to be published. I asked the publisher how many copies he expected to sell, and he said if we hit a thousand copies he would consider it a stunning success, because the public didn't normally read academic books, which are intended for experts in the field.

I discussed livelihood with Ruth. I told her we would have to lower our standard of living, and she said we'd manage. My absence was taking too great a toll, and I looked sad and tired.

We went to the beach with the kid. We hadn't done that in years, and he was ecstatic over the sun and the waves. I asked around and found a part-time job at the university—for a hunger salary, but a job nonetheless.

But then you called. Almost at the last minute, you summoned me through one of your deputies to a meeting regarding preparations for the seventy-fifth anniversary of the Wannsee Conference. Taking your honor and the magnitude of the event into account, I couldn't say no, so I drove to Jerusalem. Your deputy had explained over the phone that you were impressed with my dissertation, as well as the knowledge I'd accumulated in the field in Poland, and you thought I'd be able to contribute to the task. You said the archaeologist from Sobibor had also given them a positive report of my visit there.

I told Ruth about it, and she recognized the enthusiasm I was trying to keep at bay, and how this invitation filled me with self-importance. She was familiar with my ambition. She already knew, though I hadn't made up my mind yet. That night, just before I put Ido to bed, he handed me a drawing he'd made, of a monster with many heads and limbs painted red and black, and a small man standing tall before it.

"That's you, Dad," he cheered. "Fighting the monster!"

I arrived at the meeting early and wandered for a spell among the fragrant pines on the border of the Jerusalem Forest, with its clean dirt and clear air. By the time I walked into the conference room, officers in uniform, government officials, and Yad Vashem experts were already whispering around the coffee station.

After a slight delay, we were asked to take our seats. I took a seat at the conference table, behind a small sign with my name on it, along with the title "Poland Extermination Camp Expert." The officers across the table examined me. I was embarrassed, but proud of the position I'd achieved justly and through hard work. I was flattered. You walked in and the meeting began. "This is an initial working session," you said. "Let's see where it takes us. At this point I want to ask all of you to maintain confidentiality. In a little over a year, it will have been seventy-five years since the Wannsee Conference, which took place on January 20,

1942, chaired by Reinhard Heydrich, chief of the Reich Main Security Office. Hundreds of thousands of Jews were murdered before the conference," you emphasized, "possibly even more than a million, murdered by firing squad, by fire, by starvation, all manner of methods. Gas trucks were utilized in Chelmno even before the conference. But Wannsee is typically seen as the beginning of the Final Solution."

You told us that in light of this occasion, the Germans would be holding a conference of thinkers and artists at the villa in Wannsee. There would be, of course, Israeli representatives present, but the conference would be intellectual in nature and mostly devoted to the Germans' self-examination. Simultaneously, the Israeli prime minister had requested Yad Vashem, the Ministry of Defense, and the Ministry of Foreign Affairs to examine the possibility of holding a central memorial event at one of the extermination camps in Poland. "The prime minister is a man of historical awareness," you said, "and he believes the event should take place at the location of the murder."

Your office manager clicked a button and a presentation appeared on the screen, under the title "Israel's Show of Power at the Site of Extermination—the People of Israel Live" with a picture of the gate to Auschwitz and the famous "Arbeit Macht Frei" sign, on the backdrop of the Israeli flag. You explained that the Polish government would most likely not allow for the event to take place in Auschwitz, due to interior considerations. Our first mission, therefore, was to pick an alternate location for the event. "This could prove to be a blessing in disguise," you said. "Everyone's already heard about Auschwitz. Now we can turn the spotlight on a different central site of the Holocaust."

"What would we do there?" asked the Deputy Minister of Foreign Affairs.

The answer appeared in one of the next slides in the presentation. This would be a combined event, you explained, including elements from all of Israeli society. Though it would be mainly run by the military, it was absolutely not intended to be a military event alone. Political leaders, rabbis, artists, and youths would also participate. The keynote speeches would be given by the president and the prime minister. "The prime minister's idea," you continued—I remember you standing, erect and confident in front of the screen, pointer in hand—"is that a combined IDF force would be landing in helicopters at the chosen site, deploying and in fact taking it over, followed by a ceremony, speeches, songs, the entire program. A few years ago," you said, "the Air Force had held an aerial demonstration over Auschwitz, you've probably all heard about it. It was impressive and a great success. This is going to be even bigger, because we'll have forces on the ground too. That's the general theme of the event."

I looked at the other participants around the table and recognized in their expressions the usual preoccupation of public officials, but no hint of surprise. The idea made perfect sense to them.

"Will there be any musicians?" the Ministry of Culture representative asked. "Of course," you said. "Accompanied by the IDF Orchestra."

Then division of labor and timelines were discussed. Your office manager handed out printed tables with a breakdown of assignments, work teams, and areas of responsibility. It was agreed that in one month, team representatives would reconvene to report on their progress. I searched frantically for my name in the tables and finally found it: I was a consultant on site decision and ceremony planning.

The presentation was over and the participants asked many questions. The discussion lasted for hours. At noon trays of sandwiches and pitchers of lemonade were brought in. During this short lunch break I walked over to you and introduced myself. This was unnecessary. You immediately said, "Of course, I know who you are. Thank you for making the effort to be here today, your presence is very important."

I was filled with pride. You can't imagine how moved I was.

Your office manager, quick and energetic, asked me to follow her and introduced me to the others, both military and civilian. I shook their hands, one by one. She introduced me as Doctor. I handed out business cards and they all promised to be in touch soon.

"A very useful meeting," said the office manager, then added, "It's exciting, isn't it?"

I nodded. Indeed, yes, exciting. I liked the attention she was paying me. When I left the meeting I felt elated. I called Ruth to tell her about it. She agreed that this was an opportunity I couldn't miss and understood the national significance of such an event. We were both very good children; we could be trusted.

I returned to Poland. My datebook was still full of tours, and now this special mission was added to the agenda.

"Personal Contract Agreement Regarding the Wannsee Project." That was the title of the contract you sent me. It emphasized that we would not have an employer–employee relationship, but the fee was handsome. I signed it.

The military did not dawdle. A lieutenant colonel from the Operations Department asked that as a first step I would send them a brief review of each extermination site, presented in table form: name of site, location, historical briefing, number of Jews murdered, victims' countries of origin, uprisings, survivors, access.

I was confused about the last column: did they mean access routes for invasion, as I had learned in tank commander course? I asked and was told this required only general addressing, because they would be studying detailed topography themselves after a site was chosen. They allotted me only a few days to form my response and thanked me for my contribution to the success of this operation.

I was able to fill most of the table by heart and quickly, without having to stop and check my books. This was truly basic stuff for me—we're all professionals here, Mr. Chairman. But there were a few columns that required special attention. First and foremost, the number of Jews murdered in each camp. As we both know, this piece of data has seen some changes over time. For years, it was common knowledge that four million people were murdered in Auschwitz. Then, with time, this estimate was reduced to 1–1.5 million people, mostly Jews. On the other hand, the estimate of the number

of people murdered in Treblinka is persistently growing, and now stands at close to a million. The estimate
of the number of victims executed at shooting pits in
the former Soviet Union has also grown exponentially,
as have the estimates of other odd deaths. I filled the
table with the information known to researchers these
days and made a note of the difficulty involved in such
an assessment. I saw piles of dead bodies before my
eyes when I completed this column in the small space
allocated for each answer.

I knew the victims' countries of origin by heart, but
still checked myself to make sure I hadn't missed a thing.
I asked if a breakdown of hometowns was also required,
and was told that country of origin was sufficient. I went
through the countries of Europe, one by one, as well as
the transports coming in from North Africa, and filled
them in. I emphasized that all camps were international
in terms of countries of origin, thanks to the complex
European rail system, which allowed trains to travel
from one place to the next without special difficulty.
The manner of determining which camp each transport
would be taken to was one of the most tiresome questions in the study of Holocaust logistics. As you know,
I myself had dealt with this question quite a bit in my
dissertation.

I gave a truncated answer in the uprising column due to the limited space, but made a note that there was much to be expanded on here. I pointed out that Auschwitz and Treblinka saw uprisings initiated by the Sonderkommando when transports dwindled and the Jews working in the death facilities realized their end was near. In Chelmno, the remaining Sonderkommando rebelled on the day the camp was closed down for good. One might wonder why they didn't rebel earlier, when they had the potential of saving the lives of other Jews, those who were not part of their ranks, but I didn't write that, because the answer was obvious, a result of the most basic survival instinct of man and animal. I'd often asked myself if I would have been able to handle the awful chores of extermination (removing corpses from gas chambers, cleaning the chambers after each round, pulling teeth, setting bodies on fire, grounding large bones, etc.), thus extending my life a bit longer. The memories of survivors show that most of the Sonderkommando people had adapted to the work, and the rate of suicide among their ranks was low. I therefore concluded that I would have adjusted. I wrote in the appropriate column that in Sobibor an uprising began after Jewish prisoners of war who had served in the Red Army had arrived at the camp—people who had not lost their humanity. This uprising was especially bold and effective. In its wake, the Germans closed down the camp, afraid the escaped rebels would expose its crimes. I also saw fit to note, very briefly, lesser-known rebellions reported in certain testimonies. For instance, a transport that had arrived at Treblinka and rebelled on its way to the gas chambers. The Germans ended up killing the rebels with machine guns. Another example is the rare rebellion of a few women who spat in the faces of Germans before being pushed into the gas chambers in Auschwitz. These were wonders to me, and if I had the choice I would erect monuments to these heroines in every city of Israel. There were also escape attempts, in spite of the barbed wire and the guard towers and the armed Germans, but almost all of them had failed. I grew furious as I filled out this column.

Onward, to the survivors' column: there were thousands of survivors from Auschwitz because it had also served as a labor camp, with dozens of sub-camps. Those who passed first selection, and were incredibly lucky, and had physical and emotional stamina, survived. On the other hand, only one man survived in Belzec—Rudolf Reder, who has given testimony about what went on in the camp. He stayed there four months, one of several hundreds of Jews utilized as camp laborers as opposed to the hundreds of thousands of Jews who were murdered the very day they arrived. One day, the SS took him to his hometown of Lvov to help them carry building materials for camp maintenance. At some point the Germans left the car and he remained inside with one guard, who had fallen asleep. Reder took advantage of the opportunity and fled the car. He found shelter with a Polish woman and stayed with her until the end of the war. The story of his escape was one of the most riveting ones I'd ever heard, and I was surprised that so little has been written about it. He was enveloped in a cloud of mystery. From Chelmno, as far as anyone knows, only three Jews had escaped. There were a few dozen survivors from Sobibor and Treblinka, who had managed to run away during the uprising that broke before the camps were closed down. I wrote to Yad Vashem to find out how many of them were still alive—the military wanted to know that, too—and I was told very few.

I'm still not completely clear on the "access" column. The military could easily open a map or look at some satellite images. But I wrote down that all the camps were accessible by car, and some of them by train lines that were still active. I also included distance from Warsaw, Krakow, and Lublin.

The very next day I received a grateful response from the military and was told that the information I had provided was very helpful as a starting point for their research. Soon, they said, I would be receiving further instructions.

Late summer, at the foot of the monument commemorating the heroes of the Warsaw Ghetto, cast in bronze on a large marble plaque. The back part, facing the old Judenrat Headquarters, features an image of hunched-over Jews walking toward their death. In the front are the heroes of the uprising—young, handsome, and armed. In the copy at Yad Vashem the bare breasts of the female fighter have been covered. That was the right choice. It was disrespectful and a bad impression of French art.

I stood before a group of Ministry of Energy officials, blinking at the sun. "How many Germans were killed during the uprising?" I asked them. They provided estimates anywhere between a hundred and a thousand.

"By most reports, no more than twenty," I corrected them.

They were flummoxed. All this for fewer than twenty dead Germans?

"I have no intention of shattering the myth, only of setting the record straight," I said. "Besides," I added in a mumble, "let's see you do that, little heroes." I'm not sure they didn't hear me. That was around the time that private thoughts began falling out of my mouth.

A few of the participants whispered in the back. I asked if there was a problem.

"Why don't you say anything about the Polish?" an official in a plaid shirt asked. "Why don't you mention their atrocities? Is this a political choice? Are we cutting them slack?"

All around him people nodded, even patted his back. He was pleased with himself.

"The Polish did not carry out the Holocaust," I told him. "The Germans did. The Poles just took the opportunity to perform their pogroms, just as they had done throughout history, as part of their national pastime. They hated the Jews for crucifying Jesus, for collecting taxes for the nobles, and for being literate. Jewish women were clean because they went to the mikveh once a week, unlike Polish women. Jewish men served them strong booze at the pub, getting them nice and hammered, then charging them for it, but never drinking with them, neither laughing with them in their impoverished joy nor crying with them when they mourned. The Jews' faces remained alert as the Poles sunk into a drunken stupor, and whenever they had a free moment they put their nose in a book, reading those enchanted words, while the Poles couldn't read at all. So out of envy and stupidity, every few years they paid the Jews home visits in the middle of the night, ripping their sheets and breaking their furniture, raping their wives and daughters, sometimes even going so far as to chop off the men's limbs one by one, until that smug expression melted off their faces. Then they went out to drink. But those drunk idiots never considered murdering all Jews. That was beyond their powers of imagination or execution. The Germans were made for this historical mission. The Germans, with their determination and ingenuity, sober, scientific. To them, the Poles were also subhuman, just a step above Jews, who were not considered human at all."

"But what about the pogroms?" the man in the back insisted.

I confirmed that there had indeed been pogroms, but to compare the responsibility of the Germans to the responsibility of the Polish was a distortion of history. "Can I ask you something?" I asked him.

He nodded, surprised.

"Why is it so difficult for you to hate the Germans?" I asked. "That's what I want to know."

The man looked at his colleagues as if something was wrong with me.

We continued our tour, heading to Umschlagplatz. I could tell they were still unsatisfied with me. At some point, my chemistry with other human beings had gone awry.

For some reason, the book's publishing date was postponed, to my great chagrin. The book was based on a doctoral dissertation that had been approved and praised, and I couldn't understand why the editor was torturing me with more and more questions. This time, he wanted to know if we could cut down part of the chapter about music in extermination camps, which he thought was too long and detailed. He even added a very unkind comment, arguing that readers might get the wrong idea about life in the camps. He was specifically addressing the anecdote about Artur Gold's Treblinka orchestra. Gold was a renowned violinist and composer in Warsaw. When he descended the train at Treblinka the Germans recognized him and decided to spare his life for a few months so that he could start an orchestra. The orchestra played by the SS barracks and sometimes outside gas chambers. There were testimonies to that effect from Sonderkommandos who had fled during the uprising. What bothered the editor was that I gave a very extensive description of the orchestra's composition, as well as its repertoire, which included both famous tunes and original pieces created especially by Gold, including the Treblinka Anthem, which the Sonderkommando people sang every day: "Looking free into the world / in rows we walk to our labor / Today Treblinka is all we have / it is our fate." All the players, including Gold—the conductor—were dressed as clowns. They were all murdered in the camp's final weeks of existence, before the Germans abandoned it and plowed the land.

In my research, I examined the differences between the repertoire the Treblinka Orchestra played on the path to the gas chambers, which included some Jewish folk songs, and the purely German repertoire the orchestras of Auschwitz played, by order of the Germans. I also wrote about the Belzec Orchestra, basing my information on the testimonies of Polish neighbors and of Rudolf Reder. At Belzec, the orchestra welcomed Jews at the train station and accompanied them throughout the extermination process, which was short and matter-of-fact. The orchestra also played on Sundays during the drunken revels of German and Ukrainian staff members. We know this orchestra had six members, including an accordion player, a flutist, and a violinist, and that the members had probably changed a few times during the camp's lifetime, after some of its members were executed. Rudolf Reder reported that the orchestra had accompanied the torturous execution of the head of the Zamosc Judenrat in front of his entire community, and that immediately after that all the city's Jews were led into the gas chamber. The song played on this occasion was a big hit at the time, and its refrain was, "Everything passes, everything ends."

The editor thought this was all too broad and unnecessary, but I insisted that we leave it all in. When I wrote that chapter I was so close to seeing it, I was almost there, among them. I thought I could finally perceive the mental distortion of the Germans and the hatred of the world that was imbued in them.

The military asked me to expand on my initial report. The additional question was, *Please clarify briefly what educational and historical message pertains to each extermination camp, and if there are distinctions.* I could tell that some thought had been put into the phrasing. I took my time with a response, because I found the question interesting. The demand that I answer briefly forced me to focus my thinking. I could see the camps before my eyes, smell the forests all around them, the heavy dirt. I circled their area with my mind, experienced their remains with my senses.

I wrote that Chelmno featured precedence, improvisation, mobility, murder on wheels. The victims were taken to the train station in town, and led from there in trucks to a large mansion, where they spent the night. The next day, they were instructed to undress in order to be disinfected and receive fresh work clothes. Up until that point, they were treated rather cordially. The mansion was even heated. The Germans maintained the ruse until the very last moment to prevent any resistance. Then, when they were in their underwear, they were pointed toward a door, beyond which the trunk of the truck awaited. At this point they were shoved in with beatings and whippings. The trunk was closed and locked, and the exhaust pipe was inserted into the trunk so that the Jews were poisoned during the drive to the forest. When the truck arrived, the Jews were buried in pits by Sonderkommandos. The experts who killed tens of thousands of mental patients in Germany executed the operation in Chelmno. *What was the message of the murders in Chelmno?* I asked myself. I searched for a distinction. Most of the victims came from the Lodz Ghetto, where the head of the Judenrat, Rumkowski, rode in a decorated horse-drawn carriage. I erased this bit of information. What would the military do with it?

There was something compelling about the freshness of the Chelmno story—the boldness of misleading, the mansion that becomes a house of horrors, the Hansel and Gretel tale, the trucks riding to the meadows while their living cargo suffocates in the back. Eichmann himself came to see a demonstration there. I was so transfixed that I became disgusted with myself.

Things were much simpler when it came to Auschwitz. Many better men have written about it before me. To make my life easier and make an impression on my people in the military, I quoted a few key sayings by Primo Levi and Hannah Arendt. I also noted Giorgio Agamben but then deleted the reference, lest I appear too intellectual. In Agamben's place, I made a drawing of the burning flame at the edge of the camp, which I'd seen through the eyes of Yohanan the survivor. *Auschwitz was part murder enterprise and part financial enterprise founded on slavery till death, all in one site*, I wrote. I was pleased with this phrasing.

I wrote that Treblinka was a site for the suffocation and cremation of human flesh, a human waste removal site of enormous magnitude. Then I deleted what I'd written and refined my wording, knowing I'd been too blunt. I didn't want to lose this client. About Sobibor I initially wrote: the edge of Europe, the end of the world, among ancient forests, the end of humanity. Then I rephrased that too, to sound more practical.

Who was I writing to, I wondered. I searched for clues in the email addresses and the short messages, trying to figure out exactly how much these people knew and what exactly they were looking for. Why did they need all this information?

I wrote that almost nobody knew about Belzec, in spite of the fact that half a million people were murdered there. *Belzec represents the apex of efficiency*, I wrote in bold. Its operation was so successful that after less than a year it was deemed no longer necessary. The entire target population was annihilated, with barely any exceptions. I wrote that Majdanek was a concentration and death camp operating adjacent to a large city, exposed to anyone who drove east from Lublin on the highway—an objective presentation of Fascism. I deleted and rewrote several times, and what I ended up sending them was significantly different than what I'd initially planned to write.

I grew a dark beard during a break between tour groups. It started when I hadn't shaved for a few days, and when I looked at the mirror I seemed like a different person and decided to leave the beard. At an old clothing store near my apartment, which hadn't changed since Communist rule, I bought a dusty flat cap I saw in the window. There was a purpose to my new look: it frightened the young boys and girls, who listened more intently, and attracted teachers. In winter, I wore a heavy black coat that used to belong to my father. My mother had given it to me as a gift. When I ran into my old neighbor in the hallway she stopped and stared. She didn't recognize me, and said something in Polish.

I'm not a good neighbor, I thought. I still considered myself a tourist, when really I spent more time in Poland than in Israel. Perhaps I ought to invite her over for some tea and try to get her talking about her life, which was probably interesting, or at least had overlapped with some interesting events. About the Jews she must have known. I could ask her if she missed them. I could ask her what I looked like to her. I could pick her brain to figure out what she felt about Jews. Did she hate them? I could use her to run a psychopathological study, delving to the bottom of her old, Polish soul.

I said good morning in Polish and asked her if she wanted some tea, but she turned her back to me and rattled her keys, fleeing into her apartment, as if she thought I wanted to end her.

Talking began to weigh on me. Too many words. When I lectured, I listened to my own voice as if from the outside, like a person listening to themselves in a recording. It was grating. I had to keep my explanations short. I had to let them figure things out from the land, the forest, the silence. I read to them from Uri Zvi Greenberg's *River Streets*, as well as some chapters from Primo Levi and from Emanuel Ringelblum's ghetto journal. This was the first time they'd heard any of those. I barely looked up from the page, barely looked into their eyes. I grew more and more distant. I stood on the sidelines while they conducted their flag and candle rituals, saying the Kaddish and singing sad songs with guitar accompaniment. I tried not to listen to their conversations. I read them this poem, by Dan Pagis:

> Here in this carload
> I am Eve
> With Abel my son
> If you see my other son
> Cain son of man
> Tell him that I

That was the only way to talk. Sometimes I mustered up my strength, shook myself awake, wore an amiable expression, searched for a way in, loosened my tongue. But they closed themselves to me, refusing to accept me. Their young faces looked like a minefield to me. I sat alone in the front seat of the bus, like an unpopular child, doing my job like a robot at the different stops, which became more and more difficult. I gave them the facts, no longer thinking about education or messages. "Go," I told the driver, "keep going, we're on a schedule."

In the playground between housing projects a quick cat had hunted down a pigeon. Blond Polish children paused to watch. The pigeon twitched, fled for a moment, but the cat had already broken its wing. It dragged itself on the ground in a diagonal line while the cat trotted around it, slapping it with its paw. Feathers scattered along the path of failed escape. The mothers watched me. I was the only man there. Why wasn't I doing anything? I got up from my bench. The cat wasn't impressed with my presence, continuing to stomp its feet. Now it was biting, too. It managed to rip off the bird's head, holding it in its teeth. One boy screamed. The rest stood around, stunned. The mothers said something with a tone of complaint. I spread my arms in submission and went upstairs to my apartment.

In a response to my notes, the gaming company sent me a more advanced version of their graphic imaging. I tried it out. I played the part of a Jew, then of a German, and took some notes. The graphics were impressive. The characters were almost three-dimensional. I had wondered if they'd sent you that version too, if you had also loaded corpses into the crematorium. The flame wouldn't light before it was fed with enough human fat—that was a tip I gave them. Jews could temporarily evade death through a few options in the operating software, for instance if they'd been chosen for hard labor or a medical experiment, or if they hid in a remote corner of the camp.

The latter option did not exist in real life. I made an angry note to inform them of this. But all said, I was pleasantly surprised by their thoroughness: the game had all the components of the camp I'd described to them. They even remembered small details like gallows that had been positioned near the prisoners' sheds. I clicked my way into the latrines, which were flooded to knee height. The soundtrack played the waltzes and marches the orchestras performed each morning as the prisoners went out to work and every evening as they returned. In the undressing hall near the gas chambers, players could hear the Sonderkommandos' reassuring words and the victims mumbling in a jumble of languages. I pulled a gold tooth from the mouth of a corpse and placed it in a box. Then I switched to being German and whipped a Jew. Then I was a kapo and ladled out soup. I couldn't stop—their game was so wonderfully terrible.

On the way back from Lublin we stopped at the Izbica train station and went to see the large quad where the Germans had gathered tens of thousands of Jews in a makeshift, short-term concentration camp under the open sky before they were sent to be murdered in Belzec and Sobibor.

I told the children about Jan Karski of the Polish resistance, a handsome, elegant, blue-eyed man who had managed to sneak into the train station disguised as a Ukrainian guard, and had reported that the Jews were deprived of food and drink and forced to sleep outside. They were beaten to death and lay around on the ground, exhausted and starving, covered in their own excrement. He saw people running amok between the barbed wire fences, their malnourished children in their arms, until a train finally arrived and they were loaded into the cars with whip lashings, spear stabs, and gunshots. The train cars were filled to capacity. The Germans and Ukrainians tossed babies over adults' heads as if they were hand luggage on an airplane.

I read to the delegation from Jan Karski's report to the British and American governments, who did not see fit to bomb the train tracks leading to the camps even once they knew for certain what took place there. It wasn't their priority. People can think what they want, but it's possible they weren't too crazy about the Jews either.

In the midst of this stream of facts, someone in the group cried out. A girl said her stomach hurt. Her friends gathered around her, laying her down on the ground. They called for the delegation doctor, but he had gone ahead on a different bus. I ran over and kneeled beside her. She said she'd had pain since the previous day, but now it hurt really badly. The school principal called the other bus to give the instruction for it to return immediately with the doctor. Her friends gave her some water and washed her face. She writhed with pain, her brown curly hair spreading on the ground. Her friends rubbed her head. "It's inside," she said, "something bad is happening to me inside. Take care of me, don't leave me here."

The boys stood aside, worried. All at once, I had no complaints about them, their kind faces. Only *they* had the right to complain to *us*, for having brought them here and made them suffer.

The other bus arrived, the doctor got off, felt the girl's stomach, and said he thought it was a gynecological condition, like ovarian torsion, and that we had to take her to the hospital. We tried to call an ambulance but got no response. I ran to the train station office a few hundred meters away and yelled at the clerk to call an ambulance, we had a sick kid on our hands. I stayed there until they rang the Red Cross. I ran back and forth from the quad to the office two or three times until the ambulance arrived. When it finally came, the paramedics brought out a stretcher and carried the girl inside. The doctor and the teacher rode to the hospital with her. I told the paramedic in broken Polish to take good care of her. It was important to me that she come out unscathed. I regretted not having noticed her earlier, her sorrow, her pain. I regretted talking without listening. I wanted to walk among her friends who remained beside the tracks and apologize to them.

"Drink some water, get some rest," the Polish driver told me when we got back on the bus. "You look terrible."

In Krakow, the night before leaving for Auschwitz, with the children already upstairs in their rooms, a large group of Hasidic men walked into the hotel in top hats and long jackets. They received their room keys, and one of them, with an orange beard and kind eyes, decided to take his time. He asked for a bottle of Coke and a plastic cup and took a seat beside me.

"From Israel, correct?" he asked after saying a blessing over his beverage. "What does a Jew do in a place like this?"

I answered him and returned the question.

"We're visiting the grave of Rabbi Elimelech of Lizhensk," he said. "I come here once a year. The rabbi promised that whoever visited his grave would not leave this world without repentance, so just in case, I come every year."

He and his friends were in high spirits in spite of having just gotten off a flight. They looked nothing like our delegations, which assumed a mask of mourning from the moment they got off the plane. "What do you do at the gravesite?" I asked.

"We pray at the rabbi's synagogue," he said, "ask for forgiveness, sing, dance, eat. Everything is ready for us there, bless the Lord. The stricter ones spend Shabbat there. We stop to visit other rabbis on the way. We see Divrey Yechezkel in a place called Sieniawa, and Zera Kodesh in Ropshitz. Jews from all over the world go to Rabbi Elimelech's grave. I'm surprised to be meeting a Jew who hasn't heard of the place."

"Don't you visit the camps at all?" I wanted to know.

"No. What for?" His face fell. "What do we have to look for in those evil places? We live our lives, seeking sacredness and steering clear of filth. Torah and mitzvahs, that's what we live for. And there was once plenty of both here, and thank the Lord we are able to carry on with the tradition today."

"But that's all over," I said. "There's only death here now."

"That's not true," he said. "There were great rabbis and the largest yeshivas, synagogues, and holy Jewish life of any generation. What do you think, it's all lost? It's all here. And here." He pointed to his temple. "And we continue to enjoy their virtue, returning this place to the Torah, drying the swamps and flowing fresh water in. And that's why our prayers are heard and our sons come with us. This is where our roots are. You must know the meaning of a root. You know, my friend," he said, leaning closer, "when the Germans, may their names be expunged from history, came to Rabbi Elimelech's grave and realized an important Jew was buried there, they opened it up, wishing to desecrate it. But when they broke the stone and dug up the grave, they found the rabbi intact, as he had been in life, though he'd died 150 years earlier. The Germans were so stunned that they ran away, and the Jews of that town were saved," he concluded, uplifted, and ordered another Coke.

I pulled out my phone and quickly checked the Yad Vashem website. "That's nonsense," I told him. "That whole story you just told is nonsense. There was a ghetto there, and a Judenrat, and forced labor, and executions, and eventually the Jews were all taken to Belzec. You might want to go there; it's where your Jews are all buried."

The joy left his face. He picked up his suitcase and stood up to join his friends. "I don't know where you just read that, but it isn't true," he said, angry. "Thanks to the righteous Rabbi Elimelech not a single Jew in that town died during the war. You know what, maybe heretics did—the ones you call 'enlightened.' They may have received their punishment. Now, good night, my friend.

Perhaps one day you'll join us there and see what I'm talking about. You could witness real Jewish joy with your own eyes."

The next day, in Auschwitz, I saw them for the first time. Not through books or the computer game, but for real. "This is where the trains stopped," I explained, hearing the train pulling up, the cars opening, seeing the floodlights, feeling the panic, *where's the kid, where's the suitcase, still alive. Where are we. Where do we go now.* I stood before my group and said nothing. I could feel their frantic movement around me. The explanations would wait. I was sick of the myth, the ideas, the perverted curiosity. I tried to hear what they were saying. *Take care of the child. No, take him with you, he's so thirsty. When will they give us something to drink? Children go with mothers. I'll see you later. Let me touch you, I want to remember. Where are my wife and child. Stand up straight, no questions. Who are you, how long have you been here. When will they give my kid something to drink. And eat. Stand. Walk. Shut up.*

"Grab him," said one of the boys standing next to me. "Catch him, he's falling."

I was gone for a few seconds, I'm not sure exactly how many. I woke up with my face wet. Above me was the strange sky. I tried to get up and the world shattered.

"Run to the entrance, have them call an ambulance, he's not well," the doctor shouted above me.

"No need," I said, "I'll get up." Through sheer force of will I got myself up on my feet. My head was burning with the effort. "Let's keep going," I said. In the direction we were headed, flames jumped out of the chimney. The stage was set for my arrival, hints of odor in the midst of nature, a flock of fleshy birds resting on the grass on the border of the forest, where they all stood in a neat line, waiting their turn to walk down the stairs. *Papa will be here soon, don't worry. They're going to give us food and drink. I'm thirsty too. The people there will help us.*

"Sit down," I managed, "and I'll tell you exactly what happened. I'll give you all the facts."

The doctor sat at my feet and watched me with concern. Someone handed me a bottle of water. They were truly worried about me. I finished my speech. I took no shortcuts. *What's going on, Mama, why are you taking your clothes off? I'll take mine off too, Mama. This nice man says we're going to take a shower and then they'll give us something to eat.*

"From this hall," I could hear myself saying, "they were taken to the extermination hall, that large rectangle you see over there. They were stuffed in there, and once the door was closed behind the final person in, the job was as good as done. All that was left was cleaning up the filth afterward."

That night, we had a concluding discussion with the kids. They were going back to Israel the next day.

"What has this trip taught you?" I hated that question, but I was required to ask it. The kids were already tired, thinking about home, their rooms, their beds, grateful to have someplace to return to. The lights in the business hotel's conference room, with its wall-to-wall carpeting, blinded me. I searched for a clear voice to explain what we were doing there. I listened to them carefully, my eyes narrowed. I knew I must seem odd to them, and that they hadn't forgotten the image of me passing out in Auschwitz.

"To be strong," somebody says.

"Strong Jews."

"To be moral but strong."

"United."

"To never forget."

"To be human."

I've heard all of this before. I know it by heart.

"Okay, one last answer," the principal said, wrapping it up.

A boy sitting on the sidelines stood up. I widened my eyes and saw a tall silhouette, glasses. An athletic type. Somehow, I knew he would be saying something meaningful.

"I think that in order to survive we need to be a little bit Nazi, too," he said.

A bit of chaos ensued. Not too much, though. He was just saying to adults what they usually only say among themselves. The teacher pretended to be shocked, waiting for me to respond, to do their dirty work for them, to take care of this monster that they and their parents had nurtured.

The kid looked perfectly normal; from a good family, with a loving mother and a functioning father.

"What do you mean?" I asked.

"That we have to be able to kill mercilessly," he said. "We don't stand a chance if we're too soft."

A few of them voiced some meek protest, nothing more.

"But you're not talking about killing innocent people," the principal clarified.

The boy thought for a moment, calculated, taking his time. He wasn't one of the monkeys. Then he said, "Sometimes there's no choice but to hurt civilians, too. It's hard to distinguish civilians from terrorists. A boy who's just a boy today could become a terrorist tomorrow. This is, after all, a war of survival. It's us or them. We won't let this happen to us again."

These were the whispers from the back of the bus, no longer contained there, enhanced in the mouth of this young man. It was an opportunity I could not let slip away. "Why the Nazis?" I asked. "Why not the Americans, the Russians, the British? They were the ones that ended up winning the war."

The boy considered this. *Just don't chicken out on me now.* "Because they went all the way," he said.

The room fell silent. I lowered my head and took my time looking up again. It was a moment of silence in memory of ourselves, and I stood at attention for it. "We didn't have to bring you here," I finally said. "We could have taken you to Paris to see the wonderful streets, or to Italy to eat the best food in the world, or to London for the theater, or to Egypt for the pyramids. We could have taken you to eat candy in the markets of Marrakesh, to see a soccer match in Barcelona, or to hear singers performing tunes about broken hearts in Athens. But we brought you here, to the site of the murder. And I suppose we've accomplished our mission. We made you see that it's all about power, power, power. I'm not going to play naïve or chaste. You're right. Power. Hitting. Shooting. Annihilating the other. Because without power we're like beasts, chickens for slaughter, dependent on the graces of others who, at any moment, in a split-second decision, could chop off our heads, strangle us, strip us of our clothes and honor, abuse us in any way imaginable; make sure there's good lighting so they can take pictures of us getting torn apart, cut, penetrated, hacked to pieces; play music in the background, turning our horrendous demise into a bit of entertainment. Everything is conditional, and therefore worthless. Culture, fashion, conversation, smiling, friendship, opinions, letters, music, sports, food, love—they have no value. They are only a flimsy sugar coating. One spit in the face melts them away. Dear teachers, you can report back to your school that the message has been received. Only power. No conscience, no manners, no second-guessing. Those only challenge the soul and harm functionality. We can't allow ourselves even a moment of weakness, because everything will be taken away. We have to be a little bit Nazi. You've finally said it. You got the point, kids, well done."

Nobody else spoke. They looked away from me. When I left the room they were already beginning to strum their guitars, some classic Israeli folk songs followed by a sensitive ballad by some new rising star. They sang deep into the night, pleasing their souls. It was the end of their journey.

The editing of my book was finally complete. It was published, and you hosted a launch party for me in your auditorium, across from the Jerusalem Forest. I remember the beautiful speech you gave in my honor almost verbatim. You stood there, straight-backed and elegant, and spoke about us, those who carry the burden of memory. You praised the meticulous precision of my book, which would help readers fathom the extermination process. "Not through empty slogans," you said, "not through meaningless words, but through facts, growing clearer in all their horrendous glory as the years go by."

I said my acknowledgments. Ruth was sitting in the front row, and I could see the pride glittering in her eyes. She had made me shave my beard and dressed me up nice. My mother was sitting next to her. The room wasn't full, but I was grateful for every person who came. Then there was a short musical number by a singer I didn't know. She sang in Yiddish, accompanied by a violin.

When it was my turn to speak I did so carefully, like a man crossing a minefield. I was thinking about the fact that I still had a career to consider, and ever since that time I had passed out the ground had never felt steady beneath me. I remember someone in the back of the audience fell asleep. I told myself I could wake her up in a second, if I only spoke the way I did to the kids on the trips. But I wasn't ready for that. I still needed a little push.

After the event was over, I signed books out front. We had chosen a cover photo of the German staff at Belzec, with their long overcoats and their psychopathic faces. It disgusted me to even touch the thing, but I kept flipping the covers and writing personal inscriptions for friends and acquaintances who came to the event to honor me. I remember you pausing behind me for a moment and resting your hand on my shoulder. How I yearned for your touch. It felt like the most natural thing in the world, and the thing I'd been missing the most. It felt so good that I couldn't speak. I felt as if you truly understood me and loved me. We said goodbye. I think that was the last time I saw you in person.

As we stepped outside, Ruth put her arms around me. She was so proud, so impressed by the book and the event, all that honor, and she didn't want to stand in my way. I had to go back.

The military's initial delegation arrived in Warsaw to begin preparations for the ceremony. I was invited to meet them at the military attaché's office. Three lieutenant colonels—a commander of a helicopter fleet, the second-in-command of an elite commando unit, and a senior representative of the IDF Spokesperson's Unit, her hair gathered behind her ears, a gold wedding band around her finger, and her full face projecting strength.

The military attaché introduced me with great fanfare, calling me an authority on all matters pertaining to death camps, a doctor with years of experience. I lowered my head modestly. They came to see the potential sites for the ceremony with their own eyes, check the different parameters, and return with a recommendation for their higher-ups. The attaché updated us that the ambassador was negotiating with high-ranking Polish representatives, trying to convince them to let us have the ceremony in Auschwitz after all, but that for the time being the answer was still no, due to the military nature of the event.

"We have a terrific collaboration going with them," he explained. "We sell them weapons and hold training sessions together, as well as exchanging intel. But these symbolic affairs are very tender. One possibility is involving the Polish military in the ceremony, and that might convince them to let us use Auschwitz, but that's problematic on our end."

The Spokesperson's officer added, with the other two officers nodding in agreement, that according to the initial information they'd received from me, as well as from their own research, they'd chosen, at this stage, to focus on Majdanek and Treblinka. They had decided not to include Belzec and Sobibor out of considerations of accessibility and topography. It turned out the three of them had already been to Poland on military memorial tours, and this time wanted to focus only on operational aspects. The attaché provided us with a large embassy car, the kind I rode in with the Minister of Transportation. We had two and a half days. We were on our way the very next morning.

On the road, they wore civilian clothing so as not to draw too much attention. We conducted our business quickly and efficiently, which suited me, because it meant I didn't have to speak too much. The three of them took pictures and recorded their impressions on small laptops. The pilot checked helicopter landing strips, obstacles such as electric cables, and the nature of winds. In Majdanek he spent most of his time in the small quad outside the gas chambers, where selection used to take place, as well as on the small plain at the foot of the ash monument and the crematorium.

"We can land here," he determined, "but in winter, which is when the ceremony is slated to take place, the harsh winds might make it difficult."

Between the stops they made for observation and documentation, the pilot chatted with me, drawing more and more information out of me, to what end I did not know. He had a sharp profile, a classically Jewish face, with large eyebrows and protruding ears. For a moment, I could see him pushing a rock-laden cart while a German whipped him; pushing on, never daring to raise his hand. But now, seventy-five years too late, we were going to show them hell.

The commando officer, the name and method of action of whose unit I am familiar with but will not describe here, was always either rushing ahead or dawdling behind. He had the habits of a tracker. He was looking for access routes among the sheds—I should have told him the guards might become suspicious—as well as the borders between different areas, where the prisoners were divided by type, gender, and nationality. He remarked that we would have to watch out for the barbed wire fences, which, to this day, serve as a significant barrier. He asked if I thought the Poles would let us cut them down.

"No," I said. "They won't."

"Then we'll just have to come up with a different solution," he said.

When we climbed atop the ash hill he considered the exact positioning of the suppressive force with their machine guns, assuming this was where the helicopters would be landing.

"What exactly are you trying to take over?" I asked him.

He said that at the moment they were leaning toward the crematoriums, both because they were situated on an easy-to-spot hill and because of their symbolic meaning, though of course from a more practical standpoint the gas chambers were more important, but at this camp they were small and not impressively located.

"Who's playing the enemy?" I asked. I wanted to show him I understood a thing or two about these things.

He said that was a complicated issue. They certainly did not intend on dressing up our own soldiers like Germans, and anyway, there was no desire to fan the flames of hatred toward the Germans, who were now such close allies. "It looks like we won't have enemy staging," he said. "But as far as our forces are concerned, it's going to be a staging of an operation like any other, not just a display of force."

The female officer, who looked quite attractive in natural light, intervened to say that they were planning on demonstrating the rescuing of Jews from death. There would be a group of students the soldiers would be rescuing from inside the sheds, maybe even from the line to the gas chambers. I noticed the two other officers making a face, but they didn't dare say anything. She was the dominant one in the group. She asked to see the statue of three vultures up close. She saw it as a symbolic point of reference. Perhaps that would be the placing of the stage for speeches and performances.

I explained it was a work of art made by a Polish prisoner, and that the ashes from the burnt bodies of prisoners were surreptitiously buried underneath it. To this day, no one knows what compelled the Germans to allow the statue to be installed there at all. They had all sorts of idiosyncrasies, like those orchestras playing to people on their way to death.

The female officer's specialty was television: camera angles, lighting, that sort of thing. She told me that before enlisting for standing service, she had spent a few years working for production companies. "Think television," she kept saying.

We were standing before her like chastised children. I could only imagine what they were planning. I understood the choreography: a helicopter landing and raising dust; strong, limber soldiers jumping out and taking over the camp in a dance of battle, combat in the open field and urban warfare, running, armed, through the paths of the camp, fighting against an invisible enemy, breathing life into ashes.

They took their time, measuring and testing and photographing. A group of Israeli high school students walked by. The officers were thrilled to meet them. They asked their names and where they were from. A small crowd formed. I was perfunctorily familiar with their guide. I nodded at him in greeting.

The children opened up to them, their teeth white, their smiles healthy. The officers treated them as if they were their own, with love and not a hint of inhibition.

I stood among them with a frozen smile, searching for a way to thaw, reaching out to touch the brown curly hair of one of the girls. I didn't mean anything by it. I'd guided a hundred delegations and never touched anyone.

She turned around with a smile, thinking I was one of her friends. I recognized my mistake right away. "What are you doing?!" she barked.

They all looked at me like I was a pervert. "I'm sorry, I didn't mean it," I said.

"Then keep your hands to yourself," she blurted, upset. Then she walked away, surrounded by her friends.

The officers stood at a distance from me. Only the pilot had seen what had happened. I looked at him pleadingly. He said nothing, but his gaze was withering.

"I didn't mean anything by it," I said, coming closer. But he turned his back on me, not interested in explanations.

The kids' guide asked them to hurry up. They said an excited goodbye to the officers and walked away, wrapped in their flags.

"So sweet. You won't find young people like that anywhere else in the world," said the spokesperson's officer. "This is our true revenge. So beautiful, smart, and accomplished."

The commando officer, short and solid, said they reminded him of himself when he was younger.

The pilot said nothing, looking at me from a distance, trying to figure me out. He had me hostage now.

I looked back on the way to the parking lot, to make sure no one was chasing me. *What crime did I commit?* I thought, all of a sudden incensed. *All I did was touch a girl's hair.*

The diplomatic vehicle raced down the highway to the west. They were all lost in their computer screens, planning fighting positions and camera angles. I had nothing to do. I knew enough, and had no desire to learn anything new. I didn't want to look out the window, either. I was sick of this country's landscape.

I recalled what you'd told me when we met at the launch in Jerusalem: that I should write down my impressions as a guide. I jotted down a few thoughts on my phone, but wasn't quite prepared for the undertaking. I needed something else, and I didn't know when I would get it.

That evening, the military attaché invited the visitors to a stylish restaurant in Warsaw. The reservation was made for five: the attaché and his wife, and the three officers. It's easy to feel unwanted. I missed Ruth and Ido very much, but when I called she sounded sleepy. "He had a bad day," she said, half-asleep. "We'll talk tomorrow."

I considered punishing the delegation—not showing up to the trip to Treblinka the next day, avenging my insult by flying home first thing in the morning. Instead, I exhausted myself walking around. I passed by Janusz Korczak's orphanage in the dark. The man never married or had any children, as is the habit of those hoping to save humankind. No one would have ever blamed him for touching a girl's hair. I imagined his silhouette walking through the rooms at night, saying good night to the children, them answering him with their small voices, good night. Perhaps they loved him, or perhaps they were only in awe of him, and he knew it, and it broke his heart.

The next day, Treblinka. From there, they would drive straight to the airport, and I would have a few free days in Warsaw until the next group arrived. I couldn't wait. I searched their faces for traces of the previous day's incident and found none, so I decided to write it off, as if it had never happened.

The pilot, a nature buff, asked that we veer off the road and drive to the Vistula River, flowing calmly and broadly. We walked right to the water. Lots of birds were resting on the banks, among the trees, and the landscape stretched to the horizon. A blessed silence fell between us.

"How cruel we are to each other," the pilot said out of the blue, a tear gleaming in his eye.

I was surprised, and envious. I'd been wandering this land for three years without being able to shed a single tear. I mustered up my courage, walked over, and put my hand on his shoulder. We were standing very close, but only for a moment, until he pulled himself together and said, "Let's keep going."

We arrived at the camp a short while later. There are the tracks, there's the forest, there are the stones symbolizing the path of the Jews. I told them about the trains that came here every day and returned empty, three thousand, four thousand, five thousand people every day. I shouted like a train announcer. I couldn't keep describing it in a restrained, mournful voice anymore. I was filled with a physical rage that demanded an outlet. And what exactly were these three officers planning to do? Bomb the plowed field with the ashes buried underneath? Raid the shadows of the forest?

The officer took pictures of the memorial stones dedicated to exterminated communities. "What do you think, should we build a set here?" she asked. "We can build a few sheds for the soldiers to occupy; some guard towers, a bit of fencing? It's too empty this way. What do you think?"

The commando officer cleared his throat awkwardly and said that fighters landing in the chopper out in the open would be in a killing field. There was nothing to hide behind and nothing to occupy.

The pilot said this was not his area of expertise, and that he didn't know anything about filmmaking.

"So, what do you think?" the officer asked me directly, even smiling. "Let's hear you for a change."

"Listen," I told her. "Just listen for a second. Do you hear anything? Wind and birds. Now travel back in time. A little more, further back. The birds are still singing, the wind is still blowing, you're in the same place, and it's full of people. They arrive by train and within an hour or two they're just dead animals, burned to ashes. Focus, feel it. They're here around us, a part of nature. They came here as subhuman and left as worm food, dust, crushed bugs. Look at this insect, running at your feet, that kind of centipede. They are inside of it. It ate their ashes on its way to the forest. What could be simpler or more natural? There's no need to talk, it's easier to look at nature, breathe the air, then stop breathing, because your airways are filled with gas. These are nature games. That's why the Germans came here, east, to fertilize the earth, because it belongs to whoever works it. They're here, in this field, screaming. Listen, just listen for a moment. They're being eaten, constantly eaten, and burned, and ridiculed. Whipped on their way to be strangled as punishment for once having worn clothes and walked the streets and raised their children and cooked their food and read books and had friends. They're just miserable meat about to be burned."

The pilot walked over and said quietly, "Come on, I think we've seen enough. We've got enough information to make our decision. We can go."

"Hold on," I said, "I have more to say to you."

But he insisted that we leave. I could only take them so far. I couldn't go really deep. They remained focused on their mission. I wanted to keep explaining it to her, but our eye contact was broken. She was whispering with the two others, and they were talking about me. The treetops wavered unusually, with gusto, as if a monster was blowing on them, and the pilot led me gently to the car that was going to take us home, to Warsaw.

I said a warm goodbye to them at the airport, squeezing their hands for maybe a touch too long, insisting on kissing the female officer on the cheeks. That's not something I normally do, but I felt attached to her all of a sudden.

The pilot asked the driver to take me home and make sure I was all right.

"Write to me when you get back," I said with an odd joviality. "Don't hesitate to ask for more details, reports, whatever you want. I'm completely at the disposal of this operation, at your disposal. I hope to see you here again soon!"

I spent hours sleeping in my apartment, evening, night, morning, midday. I felt as if I had to gather my strength, but I wasn't sure what for.

I woke up a full day later to the depressing sunset of the northern countries. When I stepped outside, I ran into my elderly neighbor, as if she'd been waiting there for me. She signaled for me to hold on. I did. She walked back into her apartment, and returned with a few items of men's clothing on hangers: a few pairs of gray pants, a used jacket, two sweaters, a belt. Take it, take it, she said with her hands.

I glanced at myself, at my clothes, and realized they were quite tattered. Good God, I'd been walking around like this all this time. I thanked her and took the clothes. I invited her in for some tea, but as usual she mumbled something and walked tensely back into her apartment. The clothes smelled pleasantly old. I would definitely wear them.

Then I Skyped Ruth. She looked at my image on the phone and said I didn't look good.

My eyes were odd; my beard wild and dirty.

"When are you coming back?" she demanded. "The kids are hitting him again."

I told her I was completely swamped with the military project and the delegations, and that I would come for a few days as soon as I could.

"You can't go out to meet people looking like that," she said. "Do something about it." Then she changed her attitude and told me she saw my book at a store. "I was so proud. I convinced the salesperson to place it somewhere more prominent, so that everyone buys it."

I told her I regretted not using a more pleasant cover image, like a forest, or a Jewish child, instead of a picture of the murderers on their day of rest.

Ruth said she thought the image was good because it drew attention.

I told her I had to go; that I had a meeting with the military attaché. I knew I had something to finish there. I couldn't leave defeated. I tried on the clothes the widow had given me. They were clean and warm, and that was enough for me.

I wrote to the members of the military delegation. I also tried to get in touch with the attaché, but no one at his office answered.

I went on one more high school trip, and then my schedule cleared up. The bookings stopped coming. I called the travel agency, but felt they were evading me. Finally, the manager told me that a few schools had sent bad reviews about me, saying there were some issues, and that they'd decided to put my services on hold for the time being.

I was mad at them for doing this behind my back. I protested. No, sir, I wasn't going to be treated that way. I yelled at them. I lost my cool. I realized my reputation was ruined. Not too long ago I was the most sought-after guide for delegations to Poland, and now I was at the bottom of the list. Of course, there were also financial implications. Ruth had become accustomed to a certain lifestyle, which is why she'd accepted my prolonged absence. Now things were hopeless.

They must have been alarmed by my reaction, because the manager of the travel agency called a short while later and invited me to get involved with a new venture: day trips to Holocaust sites for general tourists.

"What are general tourists?" I asked.

She explained that meant tourists who came to Poland on vacation, not on a Holocaust tour, but still wanted to devote a day to the subject. "It'll pay off," she promised. "Instead of going on tours that last a full week you'll be able to work on day trips, and you'll make the same money."

I didn't have much choice. I waited for something big to come. I knew it would, and didn't want to miss it.

§

A few days later I reported early in the morning to one of the biggest hotels in Warsaw, across the way from Stalin's tower, where I met the Polish minivan driver. We waited ten minutes, thirty minutes, but nobody showed up. The driver went to the reception desk to ask around. Reception called up to the room and was told our party would be right down.

Almost an hour late, a group of older people showed up, eight or nine of them, wearing heavy jackets. The men had potbellies and the women wore heavy makeup and a collection of necklaces and bracelets. They lumbered loudly into the minivan without apologizing for their tardiness.

I introduced myself to them. "I'll be accompanying you on your tour of Auschwitz," I said, trying to sound formal and imbue the trip with some meaning.

They nodded gravely and then embarked on an unending conversation, a chatter with no end in sight, all about their experiences at the casino the previous night, the shopping they had done and the shopping they planned to do, the breakfast—which they said was rich but not as high quality as in other European hotels. They listed the foods they ate, discussed the shortcomings of the Polish people, their own children and their children's partners and their grandchildren, business and real estate and money, all in a constant whirlwind of babble. They were adamant about stopping for coffee and a smoke every hour and returned carrying bags from each such stop.

I tried to figure them out. Who were these people? Their conversation revealed their hometowns, but their line of work was hard to discern. One of the more dominant members of the group owned a business. He spoke at length about an employee who opened and closed the place but didn't clean it well enough at the end of the workday. He was thinking of letting him go.

Pretty soon I was missing the students and the soldiers and regretting every negative thought I'd ever had about them. In the middle of the ride one of the group suddenly leaned over, voice hoarse with cigarettes, and said, "Doctor, they told us you're a doctor, why don't you tell us a little bit about the Holocaust, about what we're going to see today."

I was glad he'd addressed me, and gave my regular introduction talk about the origins and course of the Holocaust. I was very proud of this little lecture; the epitome of summarization and precision. But they didn't have any patience for it. They had the attention span of kindergartners, and by the time I got to the invasion of Russia and the beginning of extermination by the Einsatzgruppen and local gangs, one woman called out to her friend, "Check it out, there's an IKEA here."

After that they were all too distracted, and the lecture was over. *Maybe they're right*, I thought. What's the point in all these recitations? If it is our duty to carry on living, why not live life in all its stupidity? Or maybe they were doing this on purpose, and not out of stupidity. They looked like fairly successful people, certainly more than I, who had to accompany them to make a living. We arrived at Auschwitz I. Upon their request, I took pictures of them in front of the "Arbeit Macht Frei" gate. I was beginning to like them. I led them among the brown brick structures, through the gate exhibition, the suitcases, the prostheses, and then through the first gas chamber and the crematorium beside it. I spoke little—the exhibits spoke for themselves. I can imagine they were truly shocked, but when I told them we would now drive over to Birkenau and have another hour-and-a-half- to two-hour tour, they sent over their representative—the business owner—and he said they were ready to skip the second part of the tour, it was all very interesting and very shocking, but they'd had enough, the women in particular were having a hard time, and we could head back now.

"Fine," I said right away. I was afraid of going back there too, to those things I could see there. "But you should know that's where the mass killings happened. When people talk about Auschwitz they mostly mean Birkenau. You'll be missing the most important place."

He looked at me with gravity, with compassion, placed his big palm on my shoulder, and said, "It's okay, we get it. Don't think poorly of us, we've had enough, we don't need to see any more horrors to understand. Enough. We don't need any more. And don't worry, you'll be paid in full."

I was grateful. I felt as if he wanted to save me. I told the driver we were heading back to Warsaw.

I said goodbye to the group in the late afternoon. They lumbered out of the van, exhausted from the long trip, and tipped me and the driver.

"Hang in there," they said in parting. "Buy yourself some new shoes." Then they walked cheerfully into the hotel to prepare for their evening outing. After that I guided a few more day-trip groups, but they dwindled. The travel agency said demand was low, that it was an unsuccessful hybrid.

I prepared to go home, but before I did I wanted to make one last visit to each camp, alone, just as I had done on my first trip, years ago. I had a specific plan for this final tour. I wanted to commemorate it in photos, and I knew just where and how I wanted to say goodbye.

But then I received your personal letter, the one you wrote yourself. I was so excited, my confidence returning with gusto, all my humiliations nearly forgotten. You wrote that you'd been approached by an important German director who was making a movie about the camps. He wanted a recommendation for a guide to Poland for research purposes, and wanted it to be someone working on behalf of Yad Vashem. I came to mind immediately, and the director would get in touch. Sincerely . . .

I jumped for joy. I wanted to kiss your signature. From that point on, things moved fast. The director's personal assistant scheduled a date for the tour, the price—a handsome price, at that—was settled, and I received a list of sites he wanted to visit, all within my area of expertise. I hadn't heard of him, but found plenty of essays and reviews of his work online, mostly in German. He was sixty-two years old, from a working-class family. His father worked at a steel mill, and he himself had begun his career as assistant to Wim Wenders in the 1970s before beginning to direct by himself. I found two of his old films online. Very artistic, beautiful. One took place in Hamburg and depicted the story of a merchant sailor, and the other was about a young woman from a small town who goes to the divided Berlin to study art. The films had tenderness and cruelty. The dialogue was sparse, and the story was mostly told through images. People said about him that he didn't often give interviews and refrained from revealing his private life, because he wanted to be judged for his work, not his personal biography. Still, I found out he was married to a big German theater star, who had died of a disease a few years ago, and that they had one son. I found a picture of his deceased wife. She looked like a fine woman on whose lap to rest.

I was glad to take on this mission and finally guide a man after my own heart. I told Ruth about it and showed her myself on the phone camera after having bathed, shaved, and put on a new shirt.

"You're happy," said Ruth. "I love seeing you like this."

We met at a hotel in Krakow, a very elegant one, not the vulgar kind where I stayed with my Israeli groups. The director was more handsome in real life—tall, with a bold and sensitive face. I wanted him to like me instantly. I waited for him at the hotel lobby, and he appeared right on time, with a quick step and his assistant by his side. I felt ashamed of my simple clothing, seeing as how their own clothes were made of soft, quality fabrics.

His production company ordered a car for him, a cushy Mercedes jeep, equipped with an English-speaking Polish driver. Everything had been carefully arranged for him. The car had the pleasant aroma of leather, and the director and his assistant smelled good too. They each had their distinct fabric and perfume scent, so that I could know who was coming over just by smell alone.

The three of us sat in the back seat, the director by one window and me by the other. His assistant sat in the middle. She was very tall, thin, erect. Something about her build wasn't completely proportionate, but she had a wonderful face and transparent skin underlined by a web of blood vessels.

"So, you're the doctor," the director said in English. I don't know if anyone had told him I understood German too. "We're going to have an interesting trip together."

I asked if this was his first time in Poland.

The director said he'd been there before, and left it at that.

I normally addressed my passengers by their first name, with the exception of the minister, whom I referred to as "Sir." But I didn't call the director by his name, because he didn't give me the option. I called his assistant by name—Liza.

He sprawled back in his seat, curled into a long, soft coat, and watched the road with bright artist's eyes. There was a kind of looseness about him, while I was sitting tensely on the other side of the backseat. He asked whereabouts in Israel I was from, then told me he'd been to Israel a few times and had some friends there, artists and intellectuals, whom he also sometimes met in Berlin.

"It's an interesting country," he said. He had a way of ending his statements without detail and with a small smile, as if there were hidden meaning there.

We drove out of Krakow, toward Auschwitz. That was the first stop he'd requested. Liza sat between us, watching the landscape with a far-off gaze. The heating was on in the car, so she took off her scarf. They were both very good-looking.

I started my introductions with hesitation. He listened. When I described the Germans' desire to move eastwards, he smiled for a moment. *Germans*, I always said, not *Nazis*. When I mentioned the Jews' forced cooperation with their murderers, simplifying the extermination process, he looked into my eyes.

By the time I finished my lecture we were almost there. He asked to stop by the civilian train station of the town of Auschwitz, a few kilometers away from the camp, stepped out of the car, and took pictures of the facade, the ads, and the people waiting on the platform. I stood beside him, trying to guess the theme of the film. I was very curious.

Just before we arrived at the camp, he turned to me and said, "Before we begin, I'd like to thank you for accompanying us. I know how sensitive this situation is."

I lowered my head in gratitude. It's so easy to fall into submission, like a mouse slipping into a greased trap.

The man was very thorough. I'd never had such a knowledgeable client before. Our visit at Auschwitz went on and on. We lingered at every stop: the prisoners' sheds, the dungeons, the German guards' barracks, the kapo stations, the infirmary, and the execution wall. Sporadically, he asked short and specific questions, but most of the time he observed and photographed, both stills and video.

The woman hardly spoke. She walked a little behind us, head lowered, showing no interest, as if she were already familiar with the place.

The director stopped by the torture cells in Block 11, took a close look at the cell where prisoners had stood flush up against each other without being able to sit for days, until finally they died of exhaustion, and at the other cell, where they were chained to an iron rod and beaten. I didn't have to explain the whole story to him. He seemed to have conducted rather thorough research before he came. As Liza explained, this was the final stop before production started.

We paused for a long time in the hallway, looking at the prisoners' photographs that were hung there. He stopped in front of each one in turn, looking at the subjects' faces. I walked behind him, also riveted by those faces. I told him that in the early days of the camp's activity, the Germans still bothered to take pictures of the prisoners—mostly Poles at the time—but when Jews came to be murdered they stopped, due to practical reasons. There were a few exceptions: when they documented people with characteristically Semitic features—mostly long noses—for propaganda purposes. Most of the Jews were murdered anonymously, not even registered by name, like cattle sent to a slaughterhouse, no one thinking to document them individually beforehand.

"But cattle is eaten," the director said. "Someone puts thought into their meat, seasoning them. It's a kind of homage." Then he returned to look at the images.

Liza paused far away from us, at the entrance to the hallway. The director pulled himself away from the exhibition and walked over to her. He asked her, in a German I could more or less decipher, why she wasn't walking with him, helping him. She said this was an awful place and she was having trouble being here.

"But this is the film," he said. "These are the materials; this is the job." He closed his hand into a fist.

She raised her head and closed the gap between us with long strides. Her legs were endless.

We walked into Block 10, the medical experimentation wing, and I described the medical trials held by Doctor

Carl Clauberg and Doctor Horst Schumann, utilizing new methods of sterilization through injections for women and X-rays of men's testicles, corrupting muscles and tissues for the purposes of anatomical research, studying lethal viruses by injecting them into the bodies of prisoners.

I could tell the assistant's stomach was turning, but the director held strong. "Where did Doctor Mengele work?" he asked. Something about the picture of the camp didn't make sense to him; I could tell he was concerned.

I explained that Mengele conducted most of his studies at Birkenau, and he asked me to remember to show him those sheds when we went there.

"Some Jewish doctors worked here too, right?" he asked. He had a notepad he consulted every so often.

"Right," I said. Then I mentioned some of their names. "The Germans forced them to do it."

He nodded with a kind of satisfaction.

By the time we left Auschwitz I, I was tired. The director had picked on details like no one else I'd ever seen except for myself. I assumed he would delve just as deep at Birkenau. But our schedule was busy and we had to move on. It was already lunchtime, and I was hungry. The delegations usually came with a packed sandwich lunch, in which they always let me partake, but this time there was nothing to eat. I hated buying anything at the snack bars near the exit, but I had no choice. I bought a little snack and some juice and offered them something too, but they said they were fine with just their water bottles. They'd wait for dinner.

"We'd better hurry," said the director.

I didn't like him pushing me, but I said nothing. At the gates of Birkenau I started to feel the world spinning again. I took a deep breath, a sip of juice, and told myself to be professional. I kept reminding myself that you'd sent me; that I was representing you, and that I couldn't disappoint this time.

"There, this is the famous spot," the director announced, looking ahead to the end of the tracks as if through the lens of a camera. I thought back to my first visits, standing tall and eager, performing my job flawlessly. Rather than grow accustomed to it, my nerves had only grown more exposed with the years, and they were now virtually defenseless.

The German had prepared in advance a tidy list of the parts of the camps he wanted to see: the selection ramp and the ruins of the extermination structures, the men's camp and the women's camp, the family camp, the gypsy camp, the latrine, the infirmary, the twins' shed, Gas Chamber and Crematorium 2 (Gas Chamber and Crematorium 1 were in the main camp, which we had already visited), Gas Chamber and Crematorium 3, Kanada Warehouse, where the loot was sorted, and the more remote Gas Chambers and Crematoriums 4 and 5. He also wanted me to show him where the orchestras had stood as they accompanied the prisoners' morning routine with music, the places where gallows had been installed, the exact path the Jews followed according to the outcome of their selection, and more and more. We visited each of his stops. It was like an exhausting final exam. He took pictures and asked short, focused questions. I noticed him taking some pictures of me, too, but I didn't pay any mind to it. I was even flattered to think he saw me as a worthy subject. He challenged me as no visitor ever had with the depth of his questions and the scope of his knowledge. But there wasn't a single question he asked that I couldn't answer, and that made me proud.

Once again, Liza dragged her feet behind us with an inscrutable expression. Every so often, the director asked her to come closer, and she quickened her long steps, closing the gap. The director and I worked well together there, at a pleasing pace. I pushed away the shadows of victims and their desperate chatter. I didn't want them getting in the way.

On our way to the ruins of the more remote gas chambers, those erected during the busy period of the extermination of Hungarian Jews, he noticed, just like me, the peculiar beauty of the surrounding nature, the unique birds, the flower-ringed ponds. He took some pictures. Suddenly he paused, switched his camera to video mode, and began shooting me. I walked across the grass. The sky was cloudy, and he shot me from the front. Now I was the subject.

What are you doing? I wanted to ask, but I said nothing.

"Don't worry," he said in his laborious, precise English. He must have recognized my discomfort. "I'll only use this if you allow me to."

He continued to shoot when we were standing near the ruins of the remote killing buildings and I explained how they'd operated at full capacity during the final months of the camp's existence, when the Germans tried to complete the task before their downfall. We were completely alone. No one else had gone this far. The assistant circled us slowly as he and I discussed the minutiae of the process. We were professionals.

"I want to understand everything," said the director. "Where everything was located. I want to be able to see it with my own eyes."

I felt like he was trying to steal away the only thing I

had. He bent down, picked up a lump of dirt, and felt it in his hand, rolling it between his fingers. It looked odd, but I did the same thing every time I visited.

By the time we'd hit all the stops the place was about to close. The Mercedes waited at the exit. I could see in the director's face that he was satisfied, and so was I. I'd given him what he'd come for.

They returned to their elegant little hotel in Krakow, at the foot of the turret-laden king's fortress, and I went to the cheaper business hotel across the river, where the delegations always stayed.

Early the next morning we hit the road again, Liza sitting between us again, refreshed and kind-looking. She greeted me with a polite "good morning" and a warm smile. I was curious to talk to her more, but the director's presence did not allow it. He smoked through the open window of the car, in spite of the cold, and appeared preoccupied.

"Tell me," he suddenly said after we'd been driving for a while, "can you explain why people weren't driven from the ramps to the gas chambers? Why did they have to walk for over a kilometer?"

It was a fair question, one that I'd also considered when writing my dissertation. But the answer was simple. I explained that the elderly and the ill, those who could not work, *were* taken by trucks, but that the others walked because they had just gotten off the freight trains, and the Germans wanted to convince them they'd arrived at their final destination, where they would be receiving food and housing. Had they been put back in cars, they would have realized they'd been irrevocably separated from their relatives who'd been pointed the other way during selection, and hysteria would have ensued.

He nodded. My answer had satisfied him. "That makes sense," he said. Then he muttered to Liza in German, "Smart Jew."

She glanced at me, panicked. I pretended not to have heard or understood.

We drove to Belzec. There's a point on the way there when the plane turns into the Galician hills and the beauty of nature is heartbreaking. I asked the director if he'd ever heard of S. Y. Agnon, and he shook his head. "He won a Nobel Prize," I boasted.

He said, "I haven't read his work. A man can't read it all in one lifetime. I'm still stuck on von Kleist."

When we reached the town of Belzec, on the outskirts of which lies the camp, the director asked the driver to stop and took a little stroll down the main drag, along the small shops and low facades, photographing.

I used the moments when he walked ahead of us to ask Liza, "What is he taking these pictures for? What is this film about?"

She whispered with trepidation, "I don't know exactly. He doesn't tell me everything." Her hips were wide in proportion to her height and small breasts. That was the source of the discrepancy. But it took nothing away from her beauty.

The director signaled to the driver to follow us, and we continued on foot to the camp along the train tracks. He raised his face into the sun with pleasure, letting it glint in his dark sunglasses and his hair.

We reached the thatch-roofed train station. A freight train headed to Ukraine was parked there, the driver smoking a cigarette on the platform, enjoying the sun.

The director asked Liza to pull something up on her small laptop and show me. She presented me with the picture of the German staff in their long overcoats—the same picture that was included in my book.

I smiled.

"What is it?" he asked.

I told him I'd spent a lot of time looking at that picture, too.

"We're real partners," he said in German, then asked me to lead him to the exact spot where that picture had been taken.

Not a problem. We crossed the train tracks to the small structure where the camp commander used to live. "It was here," I said.

"Stand there," said the director. He took a picture of me. I covered my face. I didn't want it.

"Stand up straight," he said. "This is important." He took another shot.

I decided I would discuss it all with him later, asking what he planned to do with the pictures.

Just like in Auschwitz, he asked me to show him the exact route the Jews took from the moment they were taken off the trains until the moment their bodies were tossed into pits, the very same day. But it's difficult to follow the path in Belzec. The camp had been plowed and strewn with black memorial rocks. We stood at the entrance, trying to reconstruct through hand gestures where everything used to be. These were my favorite moments to be near him. I felt us working like a team of pros. I told them about Rudolf Reder, who managed to escape, and about his testimony. *Mommy, I was a good boy, it's dark, it's dark.* That's what Reder heard a child yelling from inside the gas chamber.

"Hold on," said the director. "Say that again." He placed his cigarette in the corner of his mouth and started filming me. I felt like an actor. I assumed it was for a good cause, for the sake of memory, and that was the mission you'd tasked me with. I recited the words again while the tape was rolling. My eyes caught on his large hands, his belt, his boots, his lips as he said, "Look into the camera" and sent the assistant over to position me. *What are you filming here*, voices asked from beneath the ground. *Why are you reciting the final words of a murdered child to this German?*

The director asked if I'd served in the military. I had.

"A combat fighter?" he asked.

"In a tank unit."

He hummed.

I didn't like being the subject. My job is to tell the stories of other people. "Were you a soldier?" I asked.

"My biography is irrelevant," he said.

When we got back in the car the driver played quiet classical music on the radio, a Chopin waltz followed by some Bach.

"As far as you know from all your research," he said, "do you think Hitler knew about all this?"

I answered an unequivocal yes and quoted some sources I knew by heart. "But he never visited these camps," the director said.

"They were waste sites," I explained. "The Fuhrer had no reason to get his hands dirty, smell people burning, especially being a vegetarian and a clean freak."

"Still, it's curious that he never wanted to see it," he

insisted. "Why are you being so quiet?" he asked Liza in German.

"Because it's sad," she said.

"Sad is the trivial emotional response," he said. "Look at him, even he isn't as sad as you."

She looked at me awkwardly. She took my hand that was near hers surreptitiously and held onto it for a moment. It felt nice and warm.

The driver got mixed up on the way to Sobibor and I gave him directions. I could tell the director was amused, and I knew exactly what he was thinking.

When we got out of the car he asked me to walk ahead toward the camp and got the camera rolling right away.

"Why is he shooting me?" I asked Liza, who was walking beside me. I had a feeling I was being tricked.

She whispered, "We've already been here before. This is his plan."

"When were you here?" I asked.

"Six months ago," she said. This is where I started to get really confused. "But don't tell him I told you," she added urgently. "He wants everything to be spontaneous."

We walked by the pits the archaeologist had dug, which were now covered, toward the monument, at an even pace, not too quickly, as if he had a rifle at my back.

"Now stop. Tell me about the camp," he yelled from behind me. I began to recite. I couldn't say no. This is what I'd been hired to do.

Their hotel in Warsaw was on a quiet street, in an Art Nouveau building that had been beautifully restored after the war. I asked the driver to take me back to my apartment, but Liza suggested I join them for dinner at their hotel and the director agreed. "Of course," he said. "He should eat with us."

I was flattered. They went upstairs to change. I had no idea if they were sharing a room or not. I called Ruth. She asked how the tour was going and I said it was bizarre, but that I only had one more day left. I didn't say anything more. She asked if they'd paid in advance, because our account was empty, and I promised to take care of it. Ido told me about a cake they were baking. He sounded happy, for a change. I kissed him over the phone.

When I hung up, the reception clerk called me over. He said the madam wanted me to know she would be a little late, and suggested I wait at the restaurant bar.

Once again my clothes were wrinkled. After this long and harrowing day I felt out of place at that restaurant, where candles burned on the tables and patrons chatted with quiet ease. I curled up at the corner of the bar and ordered a vodka. My mind was strewn with thorns. I had no money to eat or drink there, but the bartender didn't ask me to pay right away.

When Liza arrived, wearing makeup and a short black dress, I was already feeling tipsy. The bartender nodded at her respectfully, and she asked for a cocktail and gathered me from the bar. I followed her to the table like a child. Suddenly, I realized this was my farewell to Poland meal, and I didn't want to spoil it with any negative thoughts. I would just enjoy looking at her and talking to her for as long as she let me.

She said the director had fallen asleep and might join us a little later, unless he ended up sleeping till morning. "Order anything you want," she said. "It's on him."

We laughed. She beamed at me. We drank wine and I almost forgot everything that had taken place that day, that week, the past few years, all throughout history.

She told me about her life. She was born in a village in East Germany the same year the wall fell. She told me about her parents, the years she'd spent studying art and theater in Berlin, how she met the director, and how important it was for her to work on this project, because at her parents' home the war was still a ghost that was never discussed. She also spoke about Israelis she knew in Berlin. "You're nothing like them," she said. "You're way more gentle." Her voice was young and bold, and her eyes glittered with wine. I made myself look into them in spite of my fear. Now it was my turn to tell her about myself, but I didn't want to. "When did you come here last?" I asked.

"Six months ago." She repeated the same answer she'd given me earlier. "We visited all the places you'd just taken us to."

"Then why did you come back again?"

"Because he wanted someone like you to guide us," said Liza. Then she added, "This tour is going to be part of the film."

Now I was going to cut straight to the bone. No more beating around the bush. "Someone like me. Do you mean someone Jewish?"

She answered in German, her fleshy lips forming the word. "Ja."

Laughter erupted from my belly, crude, openmouthed. I brayed with laughter. Everyone at the restaurant turned to look at me. The headwaiter came over. I hoped Liza would cry, but she just sat there, tall and stunned. The headwaiter asked assertively that I leave.

"Let go of my hand," I said when he touched me. I could have destroyed him, but I had to preserve my energy.

Liza quickly took care of the bill and followed me out to the reception area, its lights dimmed for the night. "Will you still come tomorrow?" she asked with trepidation. "I apologize, but I'm sure you can fix this. His intentions are good. You can't bail on us now; he'll blame me."

"I'll come if you tell me what the film is about," I said.

"I don't know. He's got the whole thing in his head," she said. But when I turned to leave she called me back and said, "I'll send you all his notes; everything he told me." She offered her cheek for a kiss goodbye, but I wanted all of her. I wasn't about to make do with a cheek. "See you tomorrow," she mumbled. "You'll come tomorrow, won't you?"

The old lady waited for me on our floor. She was demanding something I couldn't understand. Finally, she grabbed the ends of the coat and pulled. "Give back, give back."

"Why?" I asked. "What did I do? It's a good, warm coat."

She kept pulling until finally I took it off and handed it over. She grabbed her prey and fled into her apartment.

I knocked on her door. Perhaps she was angered by my ingratitude. I wanted to invite her over for some tea in spite of the late hour, but it would never happen.

I read the director's notes Liza had sent me on my phone. She kept her promise right away, apologizing formally for the misunderstanding and asking me to confirm I would be there tomorrow. I envisioned her sitting in bed in a short nightgown, the toenails at the ends of her long legs neatly clipped, the two of them conspiring against me.

I opened the file. Half-sentences scattered over two pages. I can only remember some of them. *The unity of fate, a shared tragedy, Leni Riefenstahl shooting the Fuhrer's visit to Auschwitz, Süss enlisting into the Israeli military, nature film on the way to Crematoriums 3 and 4, the woods, regretting Jesus, Heidegger, work tools, a banker loading corpses into the crematorium, home movies, archive, sexual lust, nudity, hair, we need a Jew! One who looks like a Jew!*

I stayed dressed. I didn't shower. I waited till morning. I arrived at the agreed-upon time outside the hotel and waited for them with the driver. It was springtime. We drove to Treblinka. On the way, I gave them the facts, and the director asked nothing. The assistant was sitting beside me, not touching me.

When we arrived I led them down the usual path, but the director asked that we veer off-site and go into the woods, she and I, holding hands, so he could film us from behind.

The assistant obeyed right away, walking over to me. I stood before the director and asked what this was for.

"It's for memory," he said. "You do what I ask, just like you hit on her at the hotel last night, do the same thing now."

"What has this got to do with the Holocaust?" I asked.

He laughed. "Oh, it's got plenty to do with it. If you haven't understood that yet, you haven't understood anything. Now, please, take her hand."

That's when I gave the first blow, hard, right in his face, a bone cracked, blood came gushing out of his nose, then another one, she screamed, no stopping, hard, full force. It's what I had to do.

I haven't heard from you since, dear Chairman. You've broken all contact with me. I mustn't complain. I have betrayed the trust you've put in me. Worse—I have defiled the holy memory. I imagine you've pushed these pages aside with revulsion long ago. They are overflowing with perversion and self-hatred and emotional vomit. What does any of this turmoil have to do with you? You look into the distance beyond your window, coolly, never letting the winds of time rattle you, keeping guard over remains of memory locked in glass cases. But know this, sir—and with this I will stop pestering you—there is a monster out there. It is alive and waiting for its time to strike again. Look at me. It has bit into my flesh, and I haven't stopped bleeding ever since.

"WE MAKE ALLOWANCES FOR OURSELVES AS IF WE WERE STILL WEAK, HELPLESS JEWS"

From an interview with Yishai Sarid
for Haaretz.com, conducted by David B. Green
November 10, 2020

MANIPULATION AND TRAUMA

Yishai Sarid's book is a critique of Holocaust education, but it's far from being a sweeping dismissal of it. It's sharply written, with a heap of irony and some mockery too. But if you're wondering whether Sarid's message is that it's time to get over the Holocaust, the answer is no.

The fifty-five-year-old is the author of six novels, the most recent of which, *Minatzahat* (*Victorious*), about a female army psychologist who's an expert in training combat soldiers to lose their natural inhibitions about killing the enemy, was published in Hebrew just as *The Memory Monster* came out in English.

His father was Yossi Sarid, the longtime Knesset member and education minister, journalist—after his retirement from politics, he wrote a regular column for this newspaper—educator and poet. He died in 2015 at age seventy-five.

Yishai Sarid lives in Tel Aviv, where he also maintains a solo practice as a civil litigator. His wife, Racheli Sion Sarid, is a critical-care pediatrician and the daughter of former Labor MK Yael Dayan (and granddaughter of Moshe Dayan). The couple has three children.

What follows are excerpts from a conversation with Sarid about *The Memory Monster*.

DAVID B. GREEN: *Your book is filled with extensive details about the Shoah, which you've obviously spent much time studying. It's clear that you've also visited the death camps in Poland. Did that include accompanying one of the youth tours you describe in the book?*

YISHAI SARID: The book is a novel, but it was important to me to get a lot of Shoah history into it, and I made an effort to ensure that that material was 100 percent accurate. What's fictional is the part that takes place in the present day.

As for the trips, I was in Poland twice for trips of this type. The first time was when I was eighteen, in 1983, when I went with a delegation of boys and girls from all over Israel. It was the year before we were drafted. I was an eighteen-year-old idiot—no, not an idiot, just a normal eighteen-year-old kid. Interested in the things that interest kids at that age. My feeling, in retrospect, was [that we] lacked emotional preparedness.

DBG: *Do you think it's a mistake to send groups of adolescents on such trips?*

YS: I think that if one wants to really understand the Shoah, there's no alternative to traveling there. You need to see these places with your own eyes—Auschwitz, Treblinka, Sobibor—to really understand the Shoah. But I'm against taking kids of seventeen or eighteen. For a few reasons: Their ability to understand is limited. They're very subject to manipulation on these trips, in terms of the lessons or messages of the Shoah. And also, there are sensitive kids who can suffer trauma. To drop all this on them, with all the horrors, that can really be hard.

DBG: *Your hero, who's nearly twice as old as that, is also very sensitive.*

YS: What my hero undergoes, day after day, is to relive the murder. These are still terrible places. The second time I went was when I was researching the book, in April 2016. I went by myself, and I spent over two weeks visiting almost all the death camps. And I came back paralyzed emotionally. It was too hard. I was then fifty-one, and at age fifty-one you understand a lot that you don't understand at eighteen.

DBG: *What sort of relationship did you have with the Holocaust growing up? How was it dealt with in your family?*

YS: The thoughts [I express in the book] are completely my own. But I got it from my father. The Holocaust was very present [in our home]. Father himself wrote a book called *Pepiczek*. It's a true story about a survivor who was one of "Mengele's twins."

Our family name was originally Schneider. They came from Poland, where they lived for generations upon generations in a small village, Rafalowka, in what is today Ukraine [and now known as Rafalivka].

My father would often tell us how, when he was five or six, his father, Yaakov Schneider—who was a teacher [and in the 1970s was director general of the Israeli Education Ministry]—went to Europe at the end of 1945, to go to displaced person camps to teach kids and prepare them for aliyah. On the eve of his departure, he decided—and Father described this very vividly, because it really stayed with him—"From this day, we'll call ourselves Sarid [Hebrew for 'survivor'], because we are the only survivors from our family." All the rest were murdered in Europe.

In his politics, my father thought we couldn't be like all the nations of the world. That we had to be better than them. That our tragedy obligated us with a special moral responsibility.

For some, because he was secular and a leftist, and such an outspoken one, he was perceived to be a "hater of the Jews," as anti-religion. But I remember seeing him on TV many years ago on the eve of Tisha B'Av, talking about the destruction of the Temple, and being surprised by his knowledge of the sources, his ability to quote from the Bible, and his knowledge of history.

I'll tell you about my father—and about myself. This may be a little bombastic, but to me, Father was the most Jewish man I knew. In terms of his connection to the sources, his ability to quote the Bible like an encyclopedia, his level of learning, and also his sense of Jewish continuity—including in the matter of the Shoah, and perhaps most important, in his sense of moral obligation. Even if he didn't believe in God, he possessed a "fear of heaven" in the sense that he felt we Jews had obligations in this world.

As far as I'm concerned, this is our culture, whether we like it or not. We can be influenced by the West, and by America and other cultures—and I do know them and I value them. But at the end of the day, our roots are in Jewish culture, with its good and bad elements. And I personally try to read and to learn as much as

I can. To the extent that the religious—not all, but the religious establishment—use Jewish culture for political purposes, and say that in order to be a good Jew you need to be right-wing, and so on and so on, is just not correct.

There's no contradiction between being on the Israeli left and Judaism. Maybe the opposite is true. Whom do we remember in the history of Israel? A few great kings. But not many. What we remember are the Prophets of Israel, that's the great legacy Judaism has given the world. And in that regard, the Israeli left is more Jewish than the right.

Sometimes, says Sarid, his father reminded him of those prophets.

HEROES AND VILLAINS

In one scene, the narrator meets with a survivor who has recently returned to Israel after many years of living abroad, hoping he might be able to speak with students about his experiences during the Shoah. Five decades after leaving the country, he remains angry at Yad Vashem, which, he says, identified him as a "kapo," and led to his being vilified and ostracized.

According to the survivor, the work he did as leader of a tunnel-digging team at the Gross-Rosen camp may have been brutal, but ultimately saved lives: "All I wanted was to buy us some time, get us a little more food, one day at a time, until it was over." But years later, when he was living in Israel, "you [meaning presumably Yad Vashem] reported me to the police, saying I was a bad kapo; that I collaborated with the Germans. Tell me, was there a single Jew who didn't collaborate?"

In this case, the narrator seems unsympathetic to the survivor. The next time he is in touch with the Yad Vashem chairman, he proposes that the institution assemble "an organized list of kapos," for the historical record. To his disappointment, the chairman responds by asking him, "'What do we need this for?'"

"I said, 'So we may know the truth; so we may enhance the difference between black and white.'

"'There is no black and white in history,' you said, writing me off."

I ask Sarid how he understood this lack of compassion on the part of his historian.

YS: This is an example of the gap between intellectual understanding and emotional reaction. After all, you understand that these people did not have any choice.

That it's not right to judge them regarding the horrible situation they found themselves in. But still, when you encounter someone like this, it's not easy to deal with [it] emotionally.

We know in the 1950s, they held trials of some kapos, and they stopped with it because they understood that it just isn't possible to judge people about what happened.

But it's more than that. You may ask, why is it so hard for our hero, why does he take it so hard? Because he keeps asking himself, what would I have done? And at the end, he thinks to himself, *I could have been a kapo. Because I would want to live.* And it really means that for all of us, even though we all think of ourselves as big heroes, that any one of us, in circumstances in which the most brutal force is applied to him, is capable of doing the worst things. And it's difficult for him—and difficult for me—to live with that understanding.

For Israelis—let's say that complexity is not our strong suit. The important, or one of the important, questions is: From what point of view do you look at it? Because, if you're weak and helpless, like the Jews were [during the Shoah], all you can do is try to survive, to find the next slice of bread, to protect your children. Or to have the strength to be able to go to work in the morning. You can't ask much more from yourself.

But we're not there anymore. We're strong, thank God, and we're independent, and we're in a completely different place. We're no longer helpless Jews, but we still make allowances for ourselves as if we were still weak, helpless Jews.

READING GROUP
DISCUSSION QUESTIONS

1. What did you think of the unnamed narrator of the book? Did you sympathize with him?

2. The narrator of *The Memory Monster* becomes an expert in Holocaust history, especially in the minutiae of how the killings took place. What did you make of his devotion to the topic? Do you think he was poisoned by his own study of horror?

3. The book takes the form of a letter addressed to the chairman of Yad Vashem, the Israeli memorial to the victims of the Holocaust. What did you make of this conceit? Is it effective? Do you find the narrator to be a reliable one?

4. Have you been to Yad Vashem, the 9/11 Memorial, or other such memorials? What was the experience like for you? What makes them successful or imperfect?

5. The narrator mentions that his boss—the chairman to whom the letter is addressed—is impressed by the narrator's knowledge but thinks that he lacks emotion and personal attention to the victims. "I'm a historian,"

the narrator thinks, "not a social worker." Is the narrator right to avoid emotion in his work? What place
does emotion have in the study of history?

6. The narrator senses in himself, and in the students he
guides through the camps, a certain admiration for
the Nazis in their undertaking of murder on a mas-
sive scale. What did you make of this aspect of the
book? Why do you think we are sometimes fascinated
by atrocity?

7. Leading one of his school tours, the narrator overhears
the students saying, "The Arabs, that's what we should
do to the Arabs." What point do you think the author
might be making here?

8. What do you make of the title of the book? In what
ways can memory be a "monster"?

9. To the extent that the book is a critique of how we mem-
orialize atrocity, what might it suggest as alternatives?

10. Would you recommend this book to everyone? Why
or why not?

ABOUT THE AUTHOR

YISHAI SARID (b. 1965) was born and raised in Tel Aviv, Israel. He is the son of senior politician and journalist Yossi Sarid. Between 1974 and 1977, he lived with his family in the northern town of Kiryat Shmona, near the Lebanon border. Sarid was recruited to the Israeli army at 1983 and served for five years. During his service, he finished the IDF's officer school training and served as an intelligence officer. He studied law at the Hebrew University of Jerusalem. From 1994 to 1997, he worked for the government as an assistant district attorney in Tel Aviv, prosecuting criminal cases. Sarid has a Public Administration Master's Degree (MPA) from the Kennedy School of Government at Harvard University. Nowadays he is an active lawyer and arbitrator, practicing mainly civil and administrative law. His law office is located in Tel Aviv. Alongside his legal career, Sarid writes literature, and so far he has published six novels. Sarid is married to Dr. Racheli Sion Sarid, a critical care pediatrician, and they have three children.

ABOUT THE TRANSLATOR

YARDENNE GREENSPAN is a writer and Hebrew translator. She has an MFA from Columbia University and is a regular blogger for Ploughshares. Her work has appeared in the *New Yorker*, *Haaretz*, Guernica, Literary Hub, Blunderbuss, *Apogee*, the *Massachusetts Review*, Asymptote, and Words Without Borders, among other publications.

RESTLESS BOOKS is an independent, nonprofit publisher devoted to championing essential voices from around the world whose stories speak to us across linguistic and cultural borders. We seek extraordinary international literature for adults and young readers that feeds our restlessness: our hunger for new perspectives, passion for other cultures and languages, and eagerness to explore beyond the confines of the familiar.

Through cultural programming, we aim to celebrate immigrant writing and bring literature to underserved communities. We believe that immigrant stories are a vital component of our cultural consciousness; they help to ensure awareness of our communities, build empathy for our neighbors, and strengthen our democracy.

Visit us at www.restlessbooks.org